Everyone wins at the game of love!

"Look at yourself, Delia. You're seventeen, and you've never been in love. Do you really want to spend your senior year alone?"

"What about you, Cain? Are you telling me that when you're making out with one of your endless string of girlfriends you don't feel alone?"

"At least I try."

"*I* try," I insisted. "I just don't succeed."

"Prove it!" Cain demanded.

"Prove *what*?"

"Show me that you really want to fall in love."

"You're crazy." I turned away from him.

"I mean it, Delia," Cain said. "I dare you to fall in love."

"Fine. I dare *you* to fall in love," I said.

"Great! Whoever shows up at the Winter Ball with his or her true love wins."

"Hey, what if we both fall in love?" I asked.

Cain reached over to take my hand. He looked me straight in the eye and said, "Then we both win."

Don't miss any of the books in *Love Stories*
—the romantic series from Bantam Books!

Love Stories

More Than a Friend

ELIZABETH WINFREY

BANTAM BOOKS
NEW YORK · TORONTO · LONDON · SYDNEY · AUCKLAND

RL 6, age 12 and up

MORE THAN A FRIEND
A Bantam Book / December 1995

Produced by Daniel Weiss Associates, Inc.
33 West 17th Street
New York, NY 10011

ISBN: 0-553-56666-0

Published simultaneously in the United States and Canada

Bantam Books are published by Bantam Books, a division of Bantam
Doubleday Dell Publishing Group, Inc. Its trademark, consisting of the
words "Bantam Books" and the portrayal of a rooster, is Registered in
U.S. Patent and Trademark Office and in other countries. Marca
Registrada. Bantam Books, 1540 Broadway, New York, New York 10036.

PRINTED IN THE UNITED STATES OF AMERICA

OPM   0 9 8 7 6

Chapter One

Delia

I'LL NEVER KNOW what changed in me that day. It could have been the incredibly blue sky, combined with the heady scent of honeysuckle in the air. It could have been the fact that I'd spent all of high school watching other people create gossip, but had never generated any of my own. Or maybe it was that I hadn't seen Cain for almost three months, and I was feeling a little giddy. Then again, maybe I just wanted to fall in love.

"You know what your problem is, Delia Byrne?"

"Yeah. The fact that you're constantly asking me if I know what my problem is," I responded to Cain Parson, my best friend, and—unfortunately—my harshest critic.

"Wrong again."

Cain shook his head and rolled over in the grass. We were having a picnic at Gambler's Pond, and I could tell Cain was getting bored with our polite conversation about how our respective summers had gone.

Spending Labor Day at the pond was kind of a tradition with us. When you're best friends with someone for more than three years, certain rituals have a way of forming, and if they're overlooked, both people start feeling like something is seriously wrong. So instead of hanging around Sherwood Forest Camp for a few days to have a good time with the other counselors, I flew home from Minnesota a couple of days early.

Not to make myself out as too much of a martyr, I also have to admit that Cain sacrificed a canoe trip with Andrew Rice in order to spend the day with me. But that didn't mean I was psyched up for one of his infamous let-me-analyze-Delia speeches. To get that point across, I sighed as dramatically as I could.

"Okay, Dr. Parson. Please enlighten me."

Cain sat up and took the blade of grass he was chewing on out of his mouth. "Simply put, you're strictly a diet iced tea kind of a girl. Even worse, it's always *lemon*-flavored—never peach or raspberry." He smiled (egotistically, in my opinion) and lay back down. He was acting as if he'd just solved the problem of world hunger, not babbled something incoherent about iced tea.

If I'd had half a brain, I probably would have put on my Walkman headphones and ignored him. But Cain has this irritating way of sucking me into his ridiculous theories.

"Is there more?" I asked. "Or should I just stop

2

drinking iced tea and assume that my senior year in high school is going to bring me fame, fortune, beauty, and true love?"

"Aha! The lady wants to know more." Cain looked out over the field and spoke in a dramatic voice. In his mind, there were probably thousands of onlookers witnessing this stimulating conversation.

"As a matter of fact, there is more," he continued. "You see, Delia, when we went to the store, you had numerous beverage choices. Even within the iced tea realm, there were at least twelve different flavors."

"So?" I prompted.

If I didn't urge Cain along when he was talking, I could end up sitting still for hours while he went off on a million tangents.

"So why didn't you choose Mango Passion? Or Lover's Fruit Punch? Or even cream soda?"

"I don't think Lover's Fruit Punch is a flavor," I said.

"You're right, but that's beside the point. The *point* is that you never act on a whim. You don't say, 'Hey, Mango Passion sounds interesting. I think I'll try it.' Instead, you plod drearily along, a diet iced tea your only companion."

"Iced tea isn't my only companion. You are."

Cain grabbed the half-empty iced tea bottle from my hand and took a huge gulp. "Deels, I'm talking in metaphor here. Work with me."

"I'm working, I'm working," I said, sighing again.

"In any situation, you take the safe route. You're

afraid to try new things. You've lived your whole life like some nun who's promised she'd follow one path and one path only. Face it—you need to branch out."

"Why?"

"Why? *Why?* Because if you did, incredible things could happen."

"Such as?" Like I said before, Cain has a way of sucking me into his theories.

"You could be an inventor—like the person who invented the change machine. You could choreograph the hottest musical on Broadway. Even more exciting, you could fall in love. Or find a boyfriend. Or at least go on a date."

I groaned. My love life, and lack thereof, was one of Cain's favorite topics. At the most unexpected moments, such as when we were studying math, I could count on him to bring up my dateless state of existence. "This equation is just like your love life," he would say. "Lots of uninteresting factors that equal zero."

I'm making Cain out to be a heartless observer of the obvious, but he wasn't. Not at all. It's just that he didn't understand how we normal people got through the day. By "normal," I mean those of us who weren't six feet tall, with black hair, blue eyes, and incredible bodies. In case you haven't guessed, that's a physical description of Cain. He also had tons of charm, endless one-liners, and an exasperating habit of making everybody like him instantly.

But what Cain was saying about fear actually

made some sense. I *am* afraid—of lots of things. Most of all, I live in terror of rejection. I mean, I've seen girls crying in the bathroom, heartbroken because some jock decided to dump them in the middle of the lunchroom. And when I look at those girls, valiantly reapplying their lipstick and heading out to the hall to make themselves available for more torture, I sympathize. Really. But I also wonder why they put themselves in that situation. Is having a boyfriend really that great? Is it worth experiencing nausea and pain every time you see that guy put his arm around another girl? According to me, no way.

I'm what my mother likes to call a prickly pear. She means I don't let anyone get too close—it's a pop psychology thing. But as I'm constantly telling my mother, I hate pop psychology. Having everyone labeled neatly, as if they're nothing more than a box of tampons or a disposable razor, seems dehumanizing. We're all different, even eccentric. Why boil our lives down to a definition in Webster's dictionary?

As Cain was saying, I'm pretty much paralyzed with fear. Then again, who isn't?

"Fear, huh?" I narrowed my eyes and studied Cain. He'd just finished a three-month stint at a nearby Christmas tree farm. I couldn't help noticing that planting trees had done wonders for his biceps and pectorals. If only teaching jazz dance to a bunch of ten-year-olds had done the same for my quads!

Cain nodded gravely. "Look at you. You're seventeen, and you've never been in love. Do you really want to spend your senior year alone?"

It was definitely time to turn the tables. "What about you, Cain? You have an endless string of girlfriends, whom you seem to pick arbitrarily. Are you telling me that when you're making out with one of them in the backseat of your car, you don't feel alone?"

"At least I try."

"*I* try," I insisted. "I just don't succeed."

Cain laughed. "You're so full of it. The perfect guy could come along, white horse and all, and you'd let him ride right by."

"Totally untrue," I said.

Unfortunately, the further this conversation went, the more I got the feeling that Cain was going somewhere with it. I wished he'd just get to the point and then let me eat my meatball sandwich in peace.

"Prove it," he said.

"Prove *what?*" I looked at the ground, wishing I could rewind the conversation. I started thinking up entertaining anecdotes about the ten-year-old girls I'd taught dance to this summer. Anything to get Cain's mind back to the realm of the impersonal.

"Show me that you really want to fall in love."

"How?"

"How do you think? By falling in love, of course."

"Cain, it's not like getting an A in history. I can't just go out and fall in love."

"How do you know if you've never tried?"

This was getting ridiculous. Cain wasn't letting up, and I could feel my face turning red. He loved to see me flustered. For some reason, he found it endearing. I found it humiliating.

"Forget it," I said firmly. I took a bite of my sandwich and turned on my Walkman. If I didn't pay attention to him, he'd get bored and give up.

Cain reached over and pulled off my headphones. I could hear Aretha Franklin's voice, sounding muffled and sort of tinny, coming from the earpieces. "I mean it, Delia. I dare you to fall in love."

Earlier, turning the tables on him had backfired. But what choice did I have? I made one more desperate attempt. "Fine. I dare *you* to fall in love. And I'm not talking about some two-week romance with the girl who works at Minsky's Pizza."

I was getting warmed up now, thinking of all the conditions I could place on Cain's falling in love. "And I'm also not talking about a few dates with Sarah Fain, that cheerleader with the big chest. I'm talking *commitment*. A meeting of the minds."

He shrugged. "Okay. You got it."

"What?" I didn't think he'd actually go through with this. I was waiting for some witty comeback that would render the whole discussion null and void.

"I dared you. You dared me. Whoever succeeds, wins." His expression was unreadable, and I was still hoping that the whole idea was a joke.

"You honestly want us to dare each other to fall in love?"

"Why not?" He crossed his arms in front of his chest, looking incredibly conceited.

But despite myself, I was getting interested in the whole concept. Maybe Cain was right. Maybe it was time that Delia Byrne showed the guys—or at least one guy—at Jefferson High what she was made of. Besides, it was our senior year. If I made a huge fool of myself, the worst that could happen was that I'd have to suffer through the rest of senior year, then never show my face at a reunion. And I probably wouldn't go to the reunions, anyway.

But if I was going to go along with Cain's crazy idea, then I wanted the stakes to be big. I wasn't about to risk getting my heart crushed just because Cain said I should.

I nodded slowly. "You're right."

"I am?" For the first time, he sounded a little uncertain.

"Absolutely. But let's make it a bet."

Cain's eyes lit up. He loved bets. "Now you're getting it, Deels. And let's make it big."

I sat up a little straighter. "Any ideas?"

"Loser has to make the winner's lunch for a month?"

I shook my head. If we were going to do this, we had to do it right. If winning didn't seem important, we'd both probably drop the whole thing and fall back into our old patterns.

He tried again. "How about the loser has to clean the winner's room once a week for a year?"

"That's hardly fair," I said. "I'm a neat freak, and you're a slob."

"Loser has to wear a Kick Me sign for a week?"

"Nah. That loses points on originality."

"Fifty bucks?"

"Come on, Parson. You can do better than that."

Cain rolled over in the grass again. He stretched out his arms and legs and closed his eyes against the bright sun. "Let me meditate for a minute," he said. "I'll come up with stakes that'll make the hairs on the back of your neck stand up."

I lay down on my stomach, resting my head on my arms. I meant to rest my eyes and focus on coming up with a bet, but I was having trouble concentrating. So while Cain silently racked his brain, I allowed my imagination to run wild.

I pictured myself at the first big football game of the year, holding a Jefferson High banner in my hands. I watched as my still-anonymous true love trotted onto the field. He'd turn, scanning the bleachers until his eyes met mine. Then he'd flash a thumbs-up before he called his team to a huddle.

I laughed at the idea. Football players weren't my style. I've always associated big-time jocks with the image of guys whipping each other with wet towels in the locker room. Not exactly my thing.

Then I pictured myself onstage, dancing *Swan Lake*. At the end of the performance, three dozen red roses landed at my feet. In my daydream, I smiled lovingly and blew a kiss to my gorgeous boyfriend. It was a beautiful scenario, except for one problem: I think *Swan Lake* is totally overrated.

Cain sat up suddenly and clapped his hands. "I've got it. If you're up for the challenge, that is."

I turned over and propped myself up on my elbows. "Try me."

"Okay. If you lose, you have to cut your hair short

9

and peroxide it blond." He looked at me, wiggling his eyebrows.

"What?" I yelped.

I figured Cain was insane. He knew perfectly well that my hair was my only good feature—it's thick and dark and long. Almost every time I was in the women's room at Jefferson, some thin-haired girl would sigh wistfully as she looked forlornly at my hair. It was my one vanity, and Cain wanted to take it away?

I guess he noticed the stricken look on my face. "What's wrong, Delia? Are you that sure you're going to lose?"

I hate pride. It makes you say and do stuff that someone without pride would realize was lunacy. In this case, pride made me agree to Cain's terms.

"All right, Mr. Too Cool to Lose. What happens if *I* win?"

"Simple. I have to get my ear pierced."

"No way! You're always talking about getting your ear pierced. It doesn't count."

"Fine. *You* think of something."

I don't have moments of brilliance often, but when I do, they tend to be truly inspired. This was one of those moments.

"If I win the bet, then you, Cain Parson, have to shave the word *loser* into your hair. To sweeten the deal, I'll even do the shaving myself." I grinned at him.

He whistled. I could tell he didn't like the prospect of his haircut proclaiming to the world at large that he was a loser. But he couldn't exactly back out. It's not his style. "Let's shake on it," he said.

We shook hands solemnly, and then I realized we hadn't come up with a time frame. We needed to allow ourselves enough time to realistically fall in love, but not so much that we'd be doddering old grandparents by the time we compared notes.

Cain must have read my mind. "We'll settle this the night of the Winter Ball," he said. "Whoever shows up with his or her true love wins."

A new thought occurred to me. "Hey, what if we both fall in love?" I asked.

He reached over and patted me on the head. "Then we both win. It's a draw."

As Cain and I packed up our food, blanket, and assorted reading material, I began to get a sinking feeling in the pit of my stomach. The next few months were going to require more than hard work and good luck—I needed a miracle.

Chapter Two

Cain

I WOKE UP Tuesday morning with one thought on my mind—that stupid bet I'd made with Delia. I never would've proposed the whole thing if I'd thought there was any way she'd go along with it. Unfortunately, whenever I'm sure that I can predict Delia's every move, she decides to do the unexpected. So now I had to fall in love.

On the surface, you might think that task would be easier for me than it would be for Delia. I've never had problems getting dates. I'm confident, and I'm anything but shy. Delia, on the other hand, likes to keep to herself. She was one of the best-looking girls in school (if not *the* best), but if anyone told her that, she wouldn't just say "Thank you" and think they were crazy. She would go off on some tangent about patronizing, condescending males who thought they could make a woman feel good by telling her something that was obviously untrue. What can I say? My best friend has a complex.

But now that she'd decided to fall in love, you could be sure she would. Delia's goal-oriented. I'd issued a challenge, and she wouldn't sleep until she had a plan. Unlike me. I had no plan and no idea how to get one.

Delia would probably look across the room in her history class, lock eyes with some loser, and fall madly in love. Meanwhile, I'd be stuck in the backseat of my car (Delia's favorite place to imagine me with a girl), making out with some very nice girl who didn't really care whether I was dead or alive. To top it off, I'd have the word *loser* shaved into my buzz cut.

As I walked into school that sunny Tuesday morning, I scanned the halls for Delia. Who knew? Maybe she'd woken up regretting the whole bet, too. If so, I'd let her off easy, and she'd never have to know my confidence had faltered. Unfortunately, she was nowhere to be seen.

"She's probably plotting a time chart for her first date, first kiss, and first 'I love you,'" I muttered.

And knowing Delia, she'd hold off on the "I love you" until just before she and her beloved walked into the Winter Ball. She has a flair for the dramatic.

I had started climbing the four, count 'em, four flights of stairs to my new homeroom when Andrew Rice, my best friend next to Delia, came bounding up beside me. Because I'd missed his canoe trip, I hadn't seen him since the Fourth of July weekend.

"Yo, Parson," he said. "Find any angels on the tops of those Christmas trees?"

"No, but I found Scrooge, in the form of my boss. He only gave me a three-hundred-dollar bonus. After I worked my butt off all summer."

"Welcome to the real world, man. That's why I work for my dad." Mr. Rice is a lawyer, and every summer Andrew works in his firm. He spends most of his time there photocopying and faxing, which would drive me to suicide.

We reached the top of the last flight of stairs. I noticed with more satisfaction than I liked to admit that Andrew was huffing and puffing. Three months of fluorescent lights and air-conditioning aren't great for building up stamina.

"Don't look now, but Debbie Jackson's at three o'clock," Andrew said, nudging me.

I groaned. Debbie had been my girlfriend for about a month the previous spring. I liked her a lot at first, but by the end she was driving me crazy. Everything she said came out as if it were a question—except for actual questions, which sounded like statements. It made me feel as though I was on a never-ending quiz show.

I thought about ducking into a locker, but she'd already seen me.

"Hi, Cain?" Debbie said, giving me a kiss on the cheek. I noticed that she looked even better than she had the year before. She'd gotten her thick blond hair cut short, and her bangs fell into her eyes in a really cute way.

"Hey, Debbie. How was your summer?" If nothing else, I'm polite. And maybe I'd been wrong about Debbie. Maybe she was my one true love, and I'd just been too caught up in punctuation to see it before.

"It was great? I worked as a kiddie-pool life-guard? How about you."

At that moment I knew there was no future for Debbie and me. Call me crazy, but I like conversations that aren't totally annoying for me to listen to. I could feel Andrew shaking with silent laughter next to me. As far as maturity goes, he's on the same level as Barney the dinosaur's fans.

"It was good. Good," I managed to say. I glanced at my watch. "Whoa. The first bell is about to ring, and we've got Mr. Maughn for homeroom."

"I understand? I had him sophomore year?" Debbie said, turning to go. "Do you want to go out sometime."

"Yeah, maybe?" Andrew answered for me. It wasn't nice, but I couldn't help letting out a little snort of laughter. My own maturity hadn't exactly evolved to the highest level, either.

Debbie gave us a strange look, then headed down the hall.

Sliding into a desk at the back of Maughn's class-room, I shook my head. I'd dated some great girls, but I'd also dated some who probably shouldn't be roaming the streets freely, much less be my girlfriend.

"Man, there are no decent women at this school," I complained to Andrew.

Andrew shrugged.

"Remember when we were in junior high? It

15

seemed as though high school was full of beautiful, exciting girls. They must have all graduated when we were freshmen."

"Cain, I've just written down the names of twenty beautiful women in the senior class, all of whom I'd like to go on dates with this year. How can you tell me we haven't got fertile soil here?"

I shook my head again. "I'm talking about someone special. Someone I could fall in love with."

"Love? Give me a break." Andrew rolled his eyes. Then he continued writing down names.

I glanced over at his notebook, scanning the list. As my eyes went down the page I mentally crossed off the girls I'd already dated. Rekindling old flames was not going to cut it. When I got to girl number eleven, my eyes widened.

"Delia?" I sort of gasped.

"Sure," Andrew said. "She fits all my criteria." He drew a big star next to Delia's name.

I just stared at the piece of paper. He'd put her between Amanda Wright and Carrie Starks. Unbelievable. It wasn't that I didn't think Andrew should find Delia attractive, intelligent, blah, blah, blah. But the idea of putting her name on some goofy list really got to me. It was as if Andrew didn't realize that Delia was unique. She didn't fit into some hormonally motivated wish list. She was a person.

"You're sick," I finally said. "You know how mad she'd be if I told her about this?" I picked up the page and rattled it in Andrew's face.

He shrugged. "Personally, I doubt Delia cares

16

much one way or the other about how I spend my time waiting for homeroom to start." He raised his eyebrows at me. "*You're* the one who's got a problem with this, Parson."

"What's that supposed to mean?"

Andrew snapped his fingers. "You're jealous."

"You're insane," I responded. For years I'd had people teasing me about secretly being in love with Delia. And none of those snide remarks ever failed to get under my skin.

At that moment the second bell rang. I slumped back in my seat, watching Mr. Maughn pull a bunch of memos out of his briefcase. He cleared his throat and started a speech about the evils of tardiness and dozing during homeroom. Having already been through three years of high school, it was a lecture I didn't need to pay much attention to. If you've heard one first-day-of-school speech, you've heard them all.

I could feel my face getting red as I thought more about what Andrew had said. It was true that I've always been pretty protective where Delia's concerned. But that's because I know what guys are like. And I don't want anyone thinking they can talk about Delia in the same lewd, crude way they talk about other girls.

After a few minutes, Maughn concluded his welcome-back-to-Jefferson-I'm-here-to-make-your-life-miserable speech. Then he started in on the roll call, another exciting aspect of homeroom.

Somewhere in the *D*'s the door opened with a bang. I watched Maughn's face tense up. Teachers always think that if they can gain control of their classroom on the first day of school, then they'll be able to glide through the rest of the year with no major problems. Maughn obviously wasn't pleased that his plan A for discipline had just been thrown for a loop.

I turned to look at the intruder. She stood a few feet inside the doorway, as if she was hesitant to move all the way into the room. Her arms were full of notebooks, one of which looked precariously close to slipping from her grasp.

Her long blond hair was tied back loosely, showing off amazingly high cheekbones and wide, round eyes. She was wearing a black miniskirt and a striped tank top. I took a deep breath, absorbing the full effect of her long, tanned legs. Suddenly Andrew's list was the last thing on my mind.

"Name?" Mr. Maughn barked.

The girl glanced quickly around the room, as if she was hoping to find sympathizers. Her eyes locked onto mine. For a split second I held her gaze. Then I smiled.

"Rebecca Foster," she said, sounding calm and unfazed by the fact that she'd just brought a roomful of people to a halt. I guess she'd sized up the situation and decided there was no need to feel intimidated.

Maughn ran his finger down the list. "Foster, Foster, Foster," he muttered to himself. He looked up. "Do you know what time it is, Ms. Foster?"

She glanced at the clock over Mr. Maughn's desk. "Ah . . . nine-eighteen?" she said.

"Yes," he said, nodding. "And the school day begins at eight–fifty–five. What's your excuse?"

She walked to the front of the room and handed him a piece of green paper. "I was in the administration office. I'm a junior transfer."

Maughn looked flustered. Everybody else was quiet. There's something about exceptionally beautiful women that tends to make people stop talking and pay attention.

"All right, then," Maughn said. "Why don't you have a seat? I'll fill you in later about what you missed."

Rebecca smiled graciously and slid behind a desk in the front row. She stared straight at Mr. Maughn, as if he were the keeper of all of life's great mysteries. I cursed myself for having sat down in the back of the room.

Maughn picked up his roster and continued where he had left off, his voice more relaxed and friendly. He must have decided to switch to plan B—make the kids like you and they'll *want* to behave.

I was so intent on studying the back of Rebecca's head that Maughn had to say my name twice before I responded. It may have been my imagination, but I could have sworn that Rebecca sat up a little straighter when I cleared my throat and said, "Here."

Andrew passed me a note, short and to the point: "Hot babe. Front and center!" Embarrassed, I tore up the note and shoved the pieces in my pocket. I wasn't about to let him make Rebecca into just another name on his list. I could tell that she had something special. And the flutter of anticipation in my stomach led me to believe that she was going to be mine. Soon.

I spent the rest of homeroom deep in thought. How should I approach her? Should I come on strong and aggressive? Sweet and shy? Since I knew virtually nothing about her, I wasn't sure how to play my cards. I had no idea what kind of guys she dated. I didn't know if she was into music, or cheerleading, or drama. For that matter, maybe she already had a boyfriend. I silently prayed that she'd transferred from somewhere far away. If that was the case, her boyfriend wouldn't be an issue.

I haven't met too many people who'd pass up a potentially good relationship just because they're supposedly in love with someone they only get to see every month or two. It's what I call summer camp syndrome. People go to camp, meet someone, and kiss under a tree or in a canoe every night. At the end of the summer, the couple declare their love and say that the year until they're back at camp will fly by. After a few letters and an awkward phone call or two, the whole thing fades into oblivion. The next year, both individuals decide they're too old for summer camp, anyway. Yes, I'm speaking from experience—although I'll never forget those starry nights with Elaine Mason.

My musings about Rebecca Foster and failed summer romances were getting me nowhere. So I decided I'd be myself—more or less—and hope for the best. That's the route I usually take with girls. Sophomore year I'd told a girl on the track team named Gina

Roslin that I was an expert at the pole vault. When she asked me to demonstrate, I almost broke my jaw by falling face first on a hard mat. That experience (as well as some wise words from Delia) made me realize that most women are incredibly attuned to bull. And once they catch on to your game, they're generally repulsed.

When the bell rang, I stayed in my seat. I was still undecided about whether or not I should go up to Rebecca. Then I heard Mr. Maughn ask her to stay for a minute so he could repeat the Jefferson High policy routine. That was my cue to make a graceful exit.

Before I turned to follow Andrew, I took a last look in Rebecca's direction. She gave me a little smile and a wave, sort of shrugging. The gesture made my spine tingle. Right then I knew I was going to win the bet.

Delia was waiting for me in the hall. We had first-period physics together. "About our bet," she started to say.

I held up my hand, cutting her off. "Don't even try to back out, Byrne," I said smugly. "I just found the girl of my dreams. You may as well get out the scissors and peroxide now."

She made a face. "Ha! I wasn't going to back out. I just wanted to tell you that I planned to draw up a written agreement. So that you don't try to weasel your way out of being branded a *loser*."

"May the best romance win," I said.

As we walked toward class I was counting the minutes until my next homeroom.

Chapter Three

Delia

EVEN ON A good day, I knew, I was going to hate having physics first period. For the next nine months I'd be laboring over impossible equations and tedious lab experiments first thing in the morning. In my opinion, no one should have to do anything resembling math before lunch.

As I sat listening to Ms. Gordon's voice droning on and on about velocity, I watched Cain's face. His expression kept changing, as if he were mulling over something that he found really amusing. I had a feeling he was thinking about our bet, and the arrogant way he was throwing back his shoulders gave me a queasy feeling.

It was so unfair. Cain had an endless stream of good luck, and I had nothing. One time he had suckered me into going with him and his grandmother to a bingo game at the senior citizens center. By the end of the night, Cain had won over a hundred bucks. When I finally won a round, the prize wasn't cash—it was one of those "My Grandma Went to Niagara Falls and All She Brought Me Was This Lousy T-shirt" shirts. After that night, Cain insisted I wear the shirt whenever his grandmother was around. Let me tell you, lime green was *not* my color!

When the bell finally rang, Ms. Gordon was in the process of handing out our first problem set. There was so much writing on the page, it looked as if the problems had already been answered. Unfortunately, that's just the way physics problem sets look.

Before we went our separate ways, Cain handed me a piece of paper he'd been doodling on during class. He'd sketched a picture of himself inside a big heart. I was on the outside of the heart, trying to poke an arrow through it. Over my head was a bubble that said, "Peroxide blondes have more fun."

"Ha, ha," I said dryly. "Is this stupid bet all you're going to think about for the next four months?"

Cain grinned and patted me on the back. "Absolutely not. Pretty soon I'll be so in love that I won't have time to gloat over my victory." He gave my hair a little tug and walked away.

I trudged to my locker with my five-pound school-issue physics textbook feeling like lead in my arms. It was barely ten o'clock, and already this was shaping up to be the worst day of my high-school career.

Putting every ounce of my strength into slamming shut my locker, I felt vibrations all the way up to my shoulder when the metal door made contact with the frame.

"Bad day at work, dear?" I heard a sickly sweet voice behind me say.

"Ellen!" I yelled. "I tried calling you five times yesterday."

"Sorry. My dad insisted that we stop at the Buffalo Bill Museum on the way back from Colorado. It added something like twelve hours to the car ride, so we didn't get back till late last night. My butt is still numb from sitting down for so long."

I laughed and gave Ellen a big hug. Next to Cain, Ellen Frazier was my best friend in the world. Incredibly tall, thin, and blond, Ellen had that waif look you always see on models in fashion magazines. But she was totally down-to-earth and didn't see herself as anything special. She was even convinced that her notable lack of a chest made her some kind of freak.

"So how was the Frazier family reunion?" I asked.

She looked up at the ceiling and made a praying gesture with her hands. "My dad and his brothers spent three days trying to outdo each other at fly-fishing during the day. At night they had these marathon chess games that were driving my mother up the wall. Meanwhile, my little cousins were going through diapers like they were air. And guess who was on baby duty?"

"In other words, it was exactly what you expected." I reached into my pocket and pulled out a black scrunchie. The humidity was already turning my hair into frizz, and I knew that if I didn't take action, my hair would wind up resembling a mop on my head. Ellen reached out for my history book so I could use both hands to put my hair back. We'd been through the same routine for the last two years.

"Yes, it was exactly what I expected," she said, nodding. "But there was one surprise windfall."

"You fell in love with your horseback riding instructor?" I asked, taking my history book back from her.

She smiled enigmatically. "Better."

Given the fact that falling in love was my top priority, I couldn't imagine what could possibly have been placed in the "better" category. "What?" I asked.

"Two words. Miracle Bra. My aunt bought me one."

I groaned. "You're an obsessed woman."

Ellen's green eyes sparkled. "Not anymore. With feminine enhancement, I finally feel like my world is coming together."

We started walking down the hall, and I turned to look at her. As far as I could tell, she looked exactly the same. "I don't want to rain on your parade, but I can't tell the difference."

"Well, I'm not actually *wearing* it right now. It was so warm this morning that I didn't want to put all that extra padding near my body. But when fall hits, I'll be ready!"

I giggled. Ellen always managed to make the most inane comment sound completely logical. It was part of what I loved about her. "I'm sure you'll put Dolly Parton to shame," I said.

She flipped her long hair over one shoulder. "Count on it. In the meantime, you'll make Jane Austen wish she'd never picked up a pen."

We were heading toward our creative writing elective, which was a class I'd been waiting to take since I was a freshman. Ellen and I both loved to write poems, and sometimes we would write stories together by taking turns writing sentences.

"And will that be before or after I win a Tony for my starring role in a hit Broadway musical?"

We'd reached Ms. Heinsohn's classroom. The door was open, and I saw her taking the desks out of their rows and arranging them in a big circle. When she saw us, she waved us in.

"Ellen and Delia. It's good to see you. You'll be great victims for my first in-class assignment. It's always so hard to get students to read their pieces to the rest of the class."

"Don't look at me," Ellen said. "I'm not reading anything out loud on the first day."

Ms. Gordon turned to me. "Delia, can I count on you?"

I shrugged. I wasn't sure I was up to the challenge. "Maybe," I said.

Ellen and I sat down next to each other in the circle. I pulled out my favorite new notebook (it had a shiny black cover and a calendar printed on the inside), and used white correction fluid to write "Creative Writing" across the front. Just as I was about to paint my pinkie fingernail with the correction fluid, Ellen nudged me.

James Sutton was sauntering into the classroom and heading straight toward our side of the circle. My breath caught in my throat for a second, and I accidentally put my hand on top of my still-wet "Creative Writing" label.

I'd had a huge crush on James Sutton since I saw him perform in a Jefferson talent show my freshman year. With long, thick blond hair, hazel eyes, and a dimple in his cheek, James had always stood out. Now he was the lead singer of a band, Radio Waves, and girls in every grade were infatuated with him. In the last three years, he'd been in several of my classes, but we'd barely spoken. For one thing, he'd been going out with Tanya Reed, a beautiful cheerleader in the class ahead of ours. And even if he'd been free, there was no way he'd have given someone like me a chance. He could have gone out with almost any girl in school.

Ellen leaned close to me. "Word has it that Tanya dumped James when she went off to college. He's single."

I forced the beating of my heart to slow down, reminding myself that I had no hope of getting James interested in me. All Ellen's tantalizing news meant was that I was going to have to get used to seeing James with his arm around a different girl . . . and not me. Hardly the thrill of a lifetime. Still, I propped my chin on my hand so that my fingers covered up the small zit on my left cheek—just in case he looked in my direction.

As much as I loved writing, I spent most of the class sneaking glances at James. The fact that he'd chosen a writing elective made him seem even more mysterious and desirable. Maybe he was the next Ernest Hemingway. His long legs were stretched out, and they cut into the circle made by our desks. I don't think I'd ever found denim so fascinating.

After Ms. Heinsohn explained the structure of a haiku poem, she gave the class fifteen minutes to write one. All I managed was my name at the top of the page. I guess Ms. Heinsohn noticed my distracted state and took pity on me, because she picked Joe Scaglia to read his poem out loud.

At one point, Ellen reached over and wrote me a note. "How's Cain?" it read. Ellen had had a blatant crush on Cain for as long as I could remember. But she never did anything about it. For one thing, she knew about Cain's history with women and didn't think he was a good bet for a boyfriend. She also had a ludicrous theory that Cain and I were destined to be together. As many times as I'd told her that I wouldn't go out with Cain if he were the last guy on earth, she'd just look at me with a little smile on her face.

During the last couple of minutes of class, Ms. Gordon gave us our assignment for Friday. We had to choose a poem, read it to the class, and then explain what we liked about it. I mentally ran down a list of my favorite poems, already thinking about what made each so important to me.

"Meet me in the lunch line," I called to Ellen as she headed toward her calculus class.

She waved in acknowledgment, and I turned to go

back to my locker. I still had two more hours of classes before I got to experience the always-nauseating cafeteria. But before I'd walked thirty feet, I felt a hand take a firm grip on my upper arm. Immediately all the blood in my body rushed to my face. Even though he'd never touched me, I had a sixth sense that when I turned around I'd be face-to-face with James Sutton.

"Yo, Delia. How've you been?" His hazel eyes were warm, and I felt almost as if I were going to swoon, just like some Victorian lady.

"Uh, good. I've been good." I hated myself at that moment. James was probably an incredible poet, and I'd just uttered the least lyrical sentences in the history of the world.

He took a step closer to me, and I could feel goose bumps rising on my arms. I shifted my books around and tried to look casual.

"How about doing me a huge favor? For old times' sake?" he asked.

I didn't know what old times he was talking about, but I was more than willing to do him a favor. "Sure," I said, without asking exactly what the favor entailed. "How can I help?"

"I don't know much about poetry. Do you think you could go over some stuff with me? Maybe show me what's good and bad, and all that?" He actually looked a little embarrassed, and my heart melted.

"No problem," I said. "But if you're not into poetry, why are you taking this class?"

He made a face and pointed in the direction of the administration office. "Scheduling conflict."

I nodded mutely. Even if James wasn't the next Hemingway, his status as one of the best-looking guys I'd ever seen hadn't changed. "I'll meet you in the library tomorrow after school," I said, as if the whole encounter were no big deal.

He gave my arm a little squeeze, then walked off in the opposite direction. As I watched every girl in the hall give him a once-over, my thoughts went back to my bet with Cain. Maybe a new day was dawning in the life of Delia Byrne. And I couldn't have cared less whether the change was happening because of planetary alignment, fate, or a mix-up in the administration office. James Sutton had asked *me* to help him with his homework.

After school, I found Cain jogging on Jefferson's quarter-mile track. He said he liked to use the school track because it was easy for him to tally how many miles he'd run. But I always thought he liked having all of the women's sports teams watch him.

He slowed down when he saw me. I knew I had a big smile on my face. It wasn't often that I got an opportunity to give Cain anything that would qualify as news regarding my love life.

"Hey, Deels." He put one hand on my shoulder, balancing himself so that he could stretch out his hamstrings. "What's up?"

"Well, I'm totally, positively sure that this won't come to anything, but James Sutton asked me to help him with a creative writing assignment." I can't say anything related to romance without putting myself down, so I was waiting for Cain to assure me that James's request was indeed significant.

For a few seconds Cain was silent. Then he put both his feet on the ground and looked at me. "James Sutton? Don't tell me you like that loser."

I couldn't believe Cain had just called James a loser. "Excuse me?" I said, my voice rising a notch. "James is gorgeous, talented, sexy . . ."

Cain laughed. "Get real, Byrne. The guy's skull could be used as storage space. Besides, he's been going out with that airhead Tanya since before he hit puberty."

I shook my head. The male inability to understand what made other guys attractive never ceased to amaze me. "For your information, Tanya is now in college, far, far away. James is available."

"Well, well, lucky you." Cain started jogging in place, and I could tell that he didn't have anything more to say on the subject.

"That's right. For once, *lucky* me. Now if you'll excuse me, I have to go to the library." I didn't add that I wanted to research some poems *before* I actually helped James with his assignment—Cain didn't understand being prepared.

I stalked off the track, my head held high. Obviously Cain was jealous. I'd gotten a head start on our bet, and he couldn't stand to think he might lose. I raced toward my car, swinging my backpack behind me.

At midnight I was tossing around in my bed, trying to think of the perfect poem for James to read in

31

class on Friday. I pictured his face lighting up when he read the words, and the way he would instantly understand why I'd chosen it. He would take my hand in his, and bring his mouth close to mine. Just as I got to the part where James gave me a passionate kiss, the phone next to my bed rang. (My parents had given in and supplied me with my own phone line when I was fourteen and prone to tie up the circuits for an average of twenty hours a day.) The sound of the bell made my heart leap. Were James and I communicating through mental telepathy?

"Hello?"

"It's me." Right away I felt like a fool. I was always glad to hear Cain's voice, but he wasn't exactly who I'd been hoping to hear from.

I looked at the clock next to my bed. "What's up? It's late."

"Yep. And guess what your awesome best friend called to tell you?"

"You've fallen in love already?" It would be just like Cain to find what he *thought* was the perfect girl in the eight hours since I'd seen him last.

"No. *Casablanca* is the late, late movie. Channel four."

"Let me call you right back." I hung up, pulled a sheet from my bed, and walked downstairs to our den, where we have both a TV and a phone. My parents were asleep, so I didn't turn on any lights. In the bluish glow of the television set, I dialed Cain's number. He picked up on the first ring.

"Humphrey Bogart just saw her for the first time. She's listening to Sam play the piano."

"I know, Cain. It's right in front of me." I settled down in our deep couch, pressing the phone to my ear. Cain and I sometimes watched movies together over the phone; even though we usually didn't say much, we liked being able to make comments to the other person when the mood struck. *Casablanca* is our all-time favorite.

An hour and a half later, I was trying to muffle my sobs in my sheet, even though Cain knew I always cried when I realized just how doomed Rick and Ilsa's love was.

"Deels, are you crying *again?* You've seen this movie, like, thirty times."

"I know," I said, wiping my eyes. "But it seems sadder every time I see it." I was whispering, because I didn't want to wake up my mom and dad.

Cain laughed softly. "You're really a romantic at heart, you know that?"

"Ha! I'm just easily manipulated by sentimental movies," I responded.

"Sweet dreams, Byrne."

"Sweet dreams, Parson." I hung up the phone and switched off the TV. As I crept back to my room I realized that I hadn't figured out which poem I should pick for James.

"It's called 'A Drinking Song,'" I said to James. "See, Yeats was creating a metaphor about drinking wine and being in love—"

33

I broke off, feeling embarrassed. Would James think that I'd picked the poem on purpose, that I was suggesting he and I were in love or something? Then I shrugged to myself. *Most* poems were about love—he wouldn't guess I had ulterior motives.

James was grinning at me. "Heinsohn's going to eat this up. She's always talking about metaphors and similes and whatever that other poetic stuff is."

"Yeah, she'll like it. We can talk about the meaning more before class . . . if you want."

He shut the poetry book and put his hand on my knee. The touch lasted only a second, but it made me tingle all over. "You're the best, Delia."

Then he stood up, the book in his hand. I watched him leave, admiring the way his faded jeans emphasized his slim hips. Would James ever look at me the way that Yeats had looked at the woman he described in his poem? For that matter, would any guy—ever? I touched my knee where James's hand had been and thought about what Cain might say: "You've got to go for it, Deels. Or else life is going to steamroll right past you."

Well, even if Cain didn't think much of James, I was going to adopt my best friend's philosophy of life. I was sick of standing on the sidelines in the game of love. Ugh! I'd definitely been reading too much poetry. . . .

Chapter Four

Cain

Thursday, October 12
9:00 P.M.

Wow. Six weeks of school have passed, but it feels more like six days. I still haven't had a real date with Rebecca, even though I've managed to talk to her several times. Just today we had what I'd call a significant exchange.

"You going to the football game tomorrow?" I asked casually.

"Why should I?" she asked.

I shrugged. "I'll be there."

She smiled this long, slow smile that made me want to grab her and kiss those red lips. "Well, then, I'd better check my schedule," she said.

In homeroom today I couldn't catch her eye. But I have a feeling she'll be at the

35

game. I think tomorrow night's the night. Delia's going to be bummed that I'm winning the bet, but that's her problem. Anyway, she won't get her head out of the clouds over James Sutton. Just because she's been helping him with creative writing assignments, she thinks she's in love. But from what she tells me, James doesn't have much to offer in the way of stimulating conversation. I accidentally-on-purpose overheard them talking in the library, and I had to bury my head in my arms to muffle my laughter:

Delia (referring to a book in her hand): "I loved 1984. Didn't you?"

James: "Yeah. Great year. I was really into skateboarding then."

Delia: "Uh, I mean the book. By George Orwell. It's futuristic."

James: "Oh, yeah. I think I just saw the movie on TV. It was about a computer named Hal, right?"

Delia: "Sure . . ."

When is she going to see that 1) all the guy has to offer is a greasy ponytail that girls go crazy over, and 2) he's still mooning over Tanya what's-her-name?

I've really got to have a talk with her. Delia's life is bordering on pathetic.

"Cain, you really have to do something about this car," Delia said as we pulled into Jefferson

High's crowded parking lot Friday night.

"Why?" I scanned the lot, looking for a space that was big enough to accommodate my 1972 Oldsmobile.

"It's disgusting. I think there's something growing in this squeeze bottle." She held up a pint-sized squeeze bottle for me to inspect. There was some green liquid sloshing around in the bottom. Then she pointedly looked at the passenger-side floor, where her feet were resting on a pile of old newspapers. There was also an assortment of change, dirty T-shirts, and empty soda cans.

"You're right. As payment for a ride to the football game, why don't you clean the car for me? I'll even drive it over to your house in the morning, just to make it easy for you."

I'd maneuvered the Oldsmobile between a small Toyota and a Fiat, and Delia was unbuckling her seat belt. "Fat chance. I'd probably end up in the hospital, a victim of some toxic thing lurking in here."

We both slammed our doors and headed toward the football field. It seemed as though every Jefferson student—past, present, or future—within a fifty-mile radius had shown up for the first Raiders game of the season.

Delia pushed us through a crowd of underclassmen who were hanging out next to the bleachers. She led me up to the top of the bleachers, where Ellen Frazier was sitting with Mike Feldman.

"Hey, guys!" Delia called. "Have you worked up some Raiders spirit?"

Ellen grimaced. "Right. I can't wait for the cheering to start. I love watching Amanda Wright shake her pom-poms."

"What a coincidence. So do I," Mike said, wiggling his dark eyebrows.

"Why do we come to these things, anyway?" Delia asked Ellen as she sat down next to me. "It's not as if we care about football."

"We're here for the same reason as every other girl," Ellen said. "We're hoping to meet our one true love in the bleachers of Jefferson High."

I tuned out Ellen and Delia's conversation and scanned the stands. Even though I didn't think Rebecca Foster was really going to be at the football game, a small part of me hoped I'd see her blond hair and ice-blue eyes in the crowd.

Rebecca and I had talked every day that week. She'd smiled at me flirtatiously, flipped her hair in a provocative way, and given me looks that seemed as if they had been designed just for me. But after homeroom, she always disappeared down the hall, and I hadn't had a chance to ask her on a date. But I knew that I would. Every time I saw her step into Maughn's classroom as if she owned the place, I knew that I wouldn't rest until I'd kissed her.

When I saw Rebecca on the other side of the bleachers, sitting alone with a football program dangling from her hand, my heart jumped to my throat. In overalls and a tight black T-shirt, I could tell from two hundred feet away that she looked incredibly beautiful. Best of all, she was alone. It was as though opportunity had literally knocked me on the head.

When I stood up, I felt Delia pull on the back pocket of my Levi's. "Where are you going? We just got here."

"Andrew's over there," I said, pointing vaguely toward the concession stand on the other side of the field. "I'm going to see what's up with him." I didn't feel like having three people give me a hard time about going to sit with a potential love interest. I wasn't totally positive that Rebecca would give me a warm reception, and if I had to come back, I didn't want to hear everybody's comments about that fact for the rest of the night.

Before anyone could protest, I climbed to the bottom of the bleachers, keeping one eye glued to where Rebecca was sitting. Just in case Delia was watching, I headed toward the concession stand and stood in line for a minute. I glanced up at the scoreboard, saw that the Raiders were ahead 7 to 0, and realized that I hadn't watched one minute of the game. Then I jogged back to the bleachers and made my way toward Rebecca.

At night, she looked even better than she did at 8:55 in the morning. Her hair was down around her shoulders, and its silky highlights shone under the bright lights of the stands. When she saw me coming in her direction, she smiled and slid over on the bench. I took that as a sign she wanted me to sit down.

"Sugar Cain. What's going on?" she said when I got close. People had called me that before, trying to be funny. Usually it made my skin crawl. But coming from her lips, the nickname kindled a warm glow inside me.

"Not much. I'm just pretending to watch the football game."

When I sat down next to her, I maneuvered myself so that our knees were touching. Even though it was just denim against denim, I felt an electric shock travel all the way up my leg.

Rebecca looked out onto the football field, then sighed. "I was going to stay home tonight, but it gets so lonely. A person can only watch so many episodes of David Letterman and *Friday Night Videos*."

I nodded, unable to believe my luck. Rebecca was obviously searching for someone to hang out with. She was probably shy and sensitive, and that was why she always left so quickly after homeroom. "Fear no more, Rebecca. Consider me your personal guide through a Jefferson High Friday night."

She giggled softly and moved a little closer. "I heard some girls saying there's a party at Patrick Mayor's house after the game," Rebecca said.

Inwardly I sighed. I'd thought maybe Rebecca and I could go get a burger or some pizza, then take a drive outside of town. Patrick Mayor was an obnoxious football player. But if Rebecca wanted to experience a Jefferson rager, I wasn't about to tell her that her wish wasn't my command. "Perfect," I said. "I'll round up some of my friends and get them to come along. You can meet a bunch of people."

"Who are your friends?" she asked.

"Well, you know Andrew Rice. He's in our homeroom."

"Right. He's a soccer player."

I nodded, surprised that she knew what sport Andrew played. He must have been trying to put the moves on Rebecca when I wasn't around. Typical. "Yeah, he's a starting forward."

"Who else?" She looked at me expectantly, and I couldn't help noticing that she had the longest eyelashes I'd ever seen.

For a second I hesitated. I felt sort of reluctant to tell her about Delia. A lot of people had the habit of misinterpreting our relationship, and I didn't want Rebecca to get the wrong idea. But if I didn't tell her about Delia, and she found out that we were best friends, it would seem even stranger. I plunged in, keeping my voice completely neutral. "Delia Byrne is my best friend. She's sitting on the other side of the bleachers with some of our friends."

Rebecca glanced across the stands. "She's not a cheerleader?"

I laughed. The thought of Delia on a cheerleading squad was almost as funny as the thought of *me* out there leading cheers. Delia wasn't the kind of girl who enjoyed putting on a short skirt and screaming out the letters of a quarterback's name to get the crowd riled. She'd rather sit back and make cynical comments about the banality of high-school life. I shook my head. "No. But she's a dancer. In the summer she teaches jazz dance at a camp in Minnesota."

Rebecca sort of wrinkled her nose. "How— neat," she said.

"Enough about Delia. Tell me more about yourself, Ms. Foster."

Rebecca was quiet for a moment, as if she were organizing her thoughts. "Let's see. I told you I'm from New York City."

"Yeah." I was trying to focus on her words, but I was distracted by the piece of blond hair that kept blowing into her eyes. I couldn't resist using my index finger to tuck the wayward strands behind her ear.

"Did I tell you that my parents moved us here because they wanted my little brother and me to have all the benefits of a suburban lifestyle?"

"Yep." I kept thinking about how silky her hair had felt against my hand. She hadn't recoiled at my gesture, which I found promising.

"Did I tell you how cute I think you are?" She bit her lip and looked at me through her long eyelashes.

I was momentarily too shocked to speak. Finally I found my voice. "No, you didn't tell me that."

She shrugged. "Remind me at the party, and I'll tell you."

I grinned, imagining Delia walking into school with her hair dyed an atrocious blond. I was well on my way to victory.

The final score was 21 to 7. The Raiders had played a great first game, and the fans were pouring onto the field to offer congratulations. I took Rebecca's hand as we wound our way through the throngs of people. I was pretty sure Delia could get a ride home with Mike and Ellen, but just in case she was waiting for me, I didn't want to leave her stranded.

She wasn't in the stands, and after circling the football field once, I didn't see her anywhere. Rebecca didn't seem to be enjoying our tour of Jefferson's sports center, so I decided to assume that Deels was perfectly capable of finding her own way.

"Can we swing by my house so I can change?" Rebecca asked as I guided her to my car in the parking lot.

"You look great right now," I said, admiring her looks for the hundredth time that night.

"Thanks. But since I don't know anybody, I'd feel better if I didn't look so scruffy." She slid into the car, putting an end to the conversation.

As we drove toward Rebecca's I realized that if she looked scruffy at the moment, she was about to look like the winner of the Miss America Pageant.

Twenty minutes later, I was sitting on the sofa in the Fosters' living room, waiting for Rebecca to come downstairs. Her parents were out, and the house was quiet. The room was large, with high ceilings and big French doors. Mrs. Foster had already had a thick cream-colored carpet laid down, and there were several paintings hanging on the walls.

"My little brother's going to destroy this carpet," I heard Rebecca say a few minutes later. She was standing at the living room doorway, and she looked amazing. Her dress was short and red, with a low neckline. Its spaghetti straps were so thin it seemed they could snap at any moment. I inhaled deeply, willing my voice not to crack.

"Good-bye, scruffy," I said.

She twirled around delicately, then took my arm. "I accept that as a compliment," she said lightly.

"Believe me, it was meant as one."

We stepped out into the unseasonably warm night, and Rebecca locked the door of the big Tudor-style house. As we walked toward my Olds her high-heeled sandals made a quiet clicking sound on the pavement. In the velvet night, each tap of her heels seemed to whisper a promise. Despite the warm air, I shivered.

By the time we arrived at Patrick Mayor's, his block was lined with cars. We parked about ten houses down and followed a stream of fellow Jeffersonians to the Mayors' front door. Before we even got to the front lawn, I could hear music pounding through an elaborate speaker system. Rebecca's grip on my hand tightened, and I gave her fingers a gentle squeeze. I could imagine how nerve-racking it would be to walk into a house full of strangers.

All of a sudden Andrew came barreling out of the Mayors' house. He was followed by a shrieking girl carrying an Uzi-style water gun. "I'm going to get you," she yelled as she shot past us.

Andrew stopped behind me, using me as a shield. "This is neutral territory," he shouted back. "Think of Cain as Switzerland."

The girl, whom I finally recognized as Carrie Starks (number ten on Andrew's wish list), put down her gun. "All right," she said. "But I'll be waiting for you inside."

Andrew came out from behind me and slapped my hand. "Is this a great party, or what?"

I managed to nod and shake my head at the same time. "It's definitely a party, I'll say that much."

Andrew bent down to tie one of his shoelaces. "Hey, what happened to you at the game? Delia said you went over to talk to me, and then you never came back. When I told her I hadn't seen you all night, she got this really crazy look in her eye and started muttering something about a bet."

Instantly I felt guilty about having left Delia behind. But there was no use worrying about it then. I'd give her a call in the morning and apologize. Instead of answering his question, I turned to Rebecca. "Andrew, you know Rebecca Foster."

Andrew looked up from his shoe, noticing her for the first time. "Of course I know Rebecca. And anyone who makes a fool of Mr. Maughn is a person I'd like to consider a friend."

Rebecca had succeeded in flustering Mr. Maughn almost every day that week. Twice he had outright contradicted himself when speaking to her.

Andrew bowed deeply toward Rebecca, then kissed her hand.

"I don't humiliate him on purpose," she insisted. "He just has a gift for saying the wrong thing at the wrong time."

Andrew and I laughed. Talk about an understatement!

"Anyway, Delia's inside," Andrew said. "She and Ellen are tearing up the dance floor."

"Really?" I didn't know why I was so surprised to hear that she was at the party. I guess it was because I usually had to drag her to any major social event. Most of the time she got irritated at parties and bugged me to take her home after half an hour.

"Yeah, man. Check it out." Andrew sprinted toward the house, shouting a greeting to everyone he passed.

As Rebecca and I followed I told her the names and a little bit about most of the kids who were milling around the front yard. She seemed to absorb every word I said, nodding her head and staring intently at whoever I was giving a rundown on.

When we got inside, Rebecca led me straight toward the music. Someone had rolled back the carpet in the Mayors' living room, and all of the couches and chairs were pushed to the side.

Just as we stepped into the room, the music changed. I heard an old Elton John song flow out of the speakers and took that as my cue to pull Rebecca into my arms. She seemed happy to be there, so I wrapped my arms even more tightly around her waist.

As we turned a little to move farther across the floor, my jaw suddenly dropped open. Delia was dancing right next to us—almost shoulder-to-shoulder.

Her eyes were closed, and her head was pressed against James Sutton's chest. I wouldn't have been more shocked if I'd seen an elephant walk into the room. Delia just wasn't the kind of person to bring attention to herself by slow-dancing (actually, they were basically just standing there hugging) in the middle of a crowded party.

When Delia opened her eyes, she caught me staring at her. I expected her to get embarrassed and pull away from James, but she didn't. She winked and flashed me a thumbs-up sign.

"Hi, Cain," she said, sounding incredibly proud of herself—as if dancing with James Sutton were the equivalent of winning the Nobel Peace Prize or something.

"Uh, hi," I answered.

"What's up, Parson?" James asked, giving me a light thump on the back. "Who's your new friend?"

For a split second I couldn't remember Rebecca's name. But it didn't matter, because Delia spoke up. "Rebecca, right? I'm Delia, and, uh, this is James."

I saw Delia pull James a little closer, as if she didn't want Rebecca to get any ideas.

"Hi, James," Rebecca answered. She didn't say anything to Delia.

There was a long pause, which I was desperate to fill. "Maybe we'll run into each other later," I said, steering Rebecca away.

"Yeah, maybe," Delia said. But she wasn't even looking at me. She was staring straight at James, and I suddenly felt as if something significant had happened—like maybe Delia was outgrowing me.

I brushed my chin against Rebecca's soft hair, having an uncomfortable vision of myself with the word *loser* shaved across the back of my head.

It wasn't a pretty picture.

*   *   *

I talked to Delia on Sunday night. "So, how's the lovely Rebecca?" she asked as soon as I picked up the phone.

"Lovely," I answered dryly. I was waiting for her to comment on what a fool she'd made of herself by plastering her body all over Sutton's.

"Wasn't Friday incredible?"

"Incredible," I said. She wasn't picking up on my signals.

"Too bad Rebecca isn't really the kind of girl you could fall in love with. Guess I'm the lead contender in the race to find the perfect mate."

"What?" I shouted. She was seriously bugging me now. "Why shouldn't I fall in love with Rebecca?"

"Didn't you see the way she was looking at James? Obviously she's got a roving eye. I just hope James doesn't ask her out. She *is* awfully pretty."

"Give me a break. Rebecca would never go out with James. He's totally inferior to me." He was, wasn't he?

Delia laughed. "Excuse me, I forgot who I was talking to. You *are* the greatest guy in the world."

"I don't need your sarcasm," I said, feeling hurt.

Delia was quiet for a moment. "I mean it, Cain. You're the best. I only need to look at your choice of best friends to realize that."

As usual, I couldn't stay mad at Delia. "Sweet dreams, Deels."

"Sweet dreams, Dr. Parson," she responded.

When I hung up the phone, I was smiling. Delia Byrne was one of a kind—thank goodness.

Chapter Five

Delia

Wednesday, October 18

Yes, yes, yes! Today was so great, I don't know if I'll ever be able to fall asleep. Before I go into details, I'd better say that until I danced with James at Patrick's party last weekend, my progress with him hadn't been too remarkable. In fact, it had been pretty dismal.

Example: After several weeks of helping James with his assignments, I was staring at him over a book of Wallace Stevens's poetry. He caught me looking and said, "What? Do I have something on my face?"

Then, before I could stop myself, I said, "Oh, I was just sitting here daydreaming about the weekend. What are you doing Saturday night?" A perfect setup, right? Wrong.

He answered, "I've got band practice."

"Oh," I answered. Then I went back to Wallace.

"So, who's your date with?" he asked after a couple of seconds.

"My date?" I gulped.

"Yeah. You said you were daydreaming about the weekend. So I assume you have a date—that's what I usually fantasize about."

"Hmm. No one you know," I answered lamely. So much for subtle hints.

A week later, James asked me how things were going with my mystery man, and I smiled enigmatically (I hoped) and said that things hadn't worked out. He didn't answer, but he sort of burned me up with his eyes. And a few minutes later, he said, "You've really changed, Delia. You used to be more like a buddy kind of girl, but now you're . . . I don't know . . . more of a woman." Then he strolled out of the library, totally unaware that my heart was pounding a mile a minute.

Then, after creative writing today, James took my hand and pulled me into an empty lab room. He took me in his arms and started dancing with me, just like last Friday night. Then he stopped and said—in these exact words—"How about we make some more music this Saturday night?"

I admit it was a corny line, but who cares? The point is, he asked me on an actual date. Of course, when I told Cain, I

was sort of stuttering, and he totally made
fun of me. But again, who really cares?
Now I just have to make it to Saturday. . . .

Have you ever noticed that life can speed up and slow down, defying any logical conception of time? Let me explain. The first three years of high school had crawled by as if time were some medieval instrument of torture. Each class seemed to last well into the twenty-first century, Friday nights dragged by, and Sunday afternoons were prison sentences at the library.

Senior year, all that changed. In the first few weeks of October, the pace of my life had become almost dizzying. Between my growing obsession with James, hanging out with Cain, and doing schoolwork, I felt as if I were in motion twenty-four hours a day. I also realized that with a little makeup, my eyes really did stand out the way Cain had always insisted they did. Plus, I was baby-sitting after school a few days a week, and getting paid (even though it came in the form of crumpled dollar bills, not smooth, professional-looking checks) made me feel like an adult.

Thursday morning I woke up before my alarm even went off. In near darkness, I stumbled to my desk and studied my almost-blank wall calendar. After I dug an old scented marker (red raspberry, to be exact) out of my desk drawer, I circled the date October 21 on my calendar. It wasn't as if I thought I'd forget when I was going out with James—I just wanted to be able to mark the days off as they passed.

When Saturday arrived (somehow I'd expected the world to end by the weekend), my stomach was totally tied up in knots. About six o'clock, I locked myself in the bathroom and actually threw up. So much for cool.

After I was done I stared at the red-circled day on the calendar. Of course, I knew I'd always think of that first day in the library as our real anniversary. From that moment on, I'd been positive (sort of . . . well, not really) that I would win my bet with Cain. He would get sick of Rebecca within a couple of months, but I would have found true love with James. During creative writing class, I'd stared at him, imagining the two of us old and gray, surrounded by grandchildren. Ellen couldn't believe how stupid I was acting; she'd never seen me so far in the clouds. For that matter, *I'd* never seen me so far in the clouds.

By eight o'clock, I was standing in front of the full-length mirror in my room. I was wearing a short black dress and black flats. My long hair floated around my face, and I'd applied dark red lipstick. When I heard a honk outside, I grabbed my purse and raced down the stairs.

"Bye," I yelled to my parents, who were watching TV in the den.

"Cain always comes to the door," my mother called.

"Cain's a dork," I called back.

James was waiting in his red Jeep. Despite the cool weather, the Jeep's top was off, and the wind had blown a few strands of hair loose from his long ponytail. He looked breathtakingly handsome, and for a moment I couldn't believe we were actually going on a date.

He leaned over and pushed open the small passenger door of the Jeep, smiling at me. I climbed in, aware that I was on the verge of hyperventilating. We'd been alone together before, but always in public places. Sitting next to James, looking at his hand gripping the gearshift, I felt as if we were the only two people in the world.

"I thought we'd go to Jon's Pizzeria," James said when I'd managed to get my shaking hands to buckle my seat belt.

"Sounds great," I responded weakly.

For several minutes we drove in silence. Above us, the stars were already twinkling. I raised my eyes and found the brightest one. *Star light, star bright, first star I see tonight, I wish I may, I wish I might . . . win my bet with Cain. I'm ready to fall in love,* I thought. For emphasis I shut my eyes and pictured the star in my mind.

When I opened my eyes, James was glancing over at me, an amused expression on his face. "I look at you, and I sigh," James said. "You're beautiful."

My heart beat quickly. James had just quoted a line from "A Drinking Song" by William Butler Yeats, the poem I'd helped him select for our creative writing assignment weeks earlier. His voice was deep and husky, sending chills down my spine.

Jon's served terrific brick-oven pizza, and it was a popular spot for dates. I'd been there a million times with both Cain and Ellen, always secretly envying the couples who sat in the booths that lined the walls of the restaurant. I knew I was beaming as James and I entered Jon's. Every girl in the place would be staring at us, wishing she were me.

James put his hand on my back as he led me to a corner booth. Even through the fabric of my dress, I could feel the heat of his hand against my skin.

"I like pepperoni," James said as we sat down.

I looked down at the laminated menu. Cain and I always ordered elaborate combination pizzas. Our favorite was eggplant, bacon, and mushroom. "Fine with me," I said.

James leaned back and folded his hands on the table. Unsure of what to say, I did the same. Suddenly he leaned forward. "So, you and Cain Parson don't have a thing going?" he asked.

I froze. "What?"

"You and Parson. Everyone at school knows you two are joined at the hip."

I couldn't help laughing. Cain had had about twenty girlfriends in the past two years alone. Did James think I was the kind of person who would put up with my boyfriend dating on the side? "Cain has lots of girlfriends, but I'm definitely not one of them. We're just friends."

James gave our order to the waitress, then raised his eyebrows at me. "I don't think members of the opposite sex can be friends," he said. "There's always that . . . tension."

"Not in my case," I said quickly.

I was desperate to change the subject, but at the

same time I was curious about what people thought about my friendship with Cain. Did everyone believe I was in love with him? Did they assume I just sat by patiently while he went out with every other girl in school? It was a humiliating notion. I had always thought of myself as strong and unflappable—not the kind of woman to accept second place. But maybe that wasn't how others saw me. Maybe they considered me a lovesick puppy.

"Well, I know one thing," James said, taking my hand.

"What?" My thoughts about Cain flew out of my mind as I felt his strong fingers clasp mine.

"We could never be friends." His hazel eyes were glittering, and his red lips looked irresistible.

"Why?" I whispered.

"Because I'd always want to kiss you, like I want to right now."

Just then the waitress came back with our sodas. Her arrival broke the tension, but I was sure that my cheeks were flaming red. I wasn't sure how to take everything that James was saying. On the one hand, I'd barely let myself dream about this moment. On the other, it didn't feel quite real. I'd always thought that a blossoming romance would be something of a roller-coaster ride. I'd pictured myself anxiously awaiting poetic words and smoldering looks. But without really even knowing me, James seemed willing to get incredibly personal. Did he really mean what he was saying?

A few minutes later the waitress placed our pizza

on the table in front of us. As I watched James fold a slice of pizza and take a huge bite, a thought plagued me. If James was as great as I thought he was, why would he want me? After all, no one else did.

Even though my stomach was still full of butterflies, I took a slice of pizza. With James staring at me intently, I practically gagged on all the cheese. It was sliding down my throat so that I could barely breathe. I coughed, then took a huge swallow of my diet cola. I figured that if James had been attracted to me before, I'd probably just ruined any chance I had. The thought gave me an odd feeling of excitement. I'd always loved a challenge.

"So, James, what do you think of creative writing class nowadays?" I asked, desperate to move to a safer topic of conversation.

"Writing is actually pretty cool," James replied.

"You think so?"

"Yeah. I think I'm going to write some of the lyrics for my band. Mark usually does them, but his poems are pretty stupid." He took another slice of pizza and grabbed a napkin.

"That's great. I'd love to read your lyrics sometime—if you want me to, I mean."

"Maybe I'll write a song about you."

Again I felt myself blush. I looked down at my food and concentrated on eating. I wasn't any good at flirting, and no matter how much I racked my brain, I couldn't think of anything cute to say back.

James seemed content to eat in silence, so I let myself tune in to the other conversations in the restaurant. Whenever I was nervous, I found it helpful to focus on something besides myself. It was a trick my mother had taught me.

I listened in on what the people in the booth behind us were talking about. The first voice I heard belonged to a preppy-looking girl I'd seen when we walked into Jon's.

"Daddy took away my charge card for the month. He freaked out when I bought a new leather jacket last week. He's *such* an ogre."

I rolled my eyes. If I'd used my dad's charge card, I'd have wound up sitting in my room for a year.

"How unfair," the guy with her said. "Doesn't he know that without that card you're virtually a nonperson?"

"What can I do? He doesn't understand what it's like to be young. Maybe I should sue him for negligence."

I giggled out loud. The couple behind us sounded like characters out of a B movie. Were they for real?

"Are you listening to that couple?" I whispered to James.

He shook his head. "What're they saying?"

I cleared my throat and got ready to do what I called my rich-girl voice. It was a combination of Mrs. Howell from *Gilligan's Island* and what I imagined an English aristocrat would sound like.

"It's *sooo* atrocious," I said, imitating the girl. "Daddy took away my Rolls Royce. He's making me drive the Beamer. It's *sooo* humiliating." I laughed again.

James's expression was totally blank. Hearing the couple's voices again, I stopped talking. "Listen," I said, jerking my head toward the back of the booth.

"I just love what they've done with the country club. Although the mahogany paneling in the grill is a bit overdone," the girl said.

I winked at James, but he was just looking at me as if I were crazy. Obviously he didn't think my imitation was funny. I sighed. If Cain had been with me, I would have been the girl while he imitated the guy. We probably would've spent the rest of dinner role-playing—laughing hysterically the entire time.

Looking at James's serious face, I was embarrassed. It wasn't very nice of me to be making fun of other people. I decided that for Buffy (I'd mentally named the girl Buffy), having her dad take away her credit card probably *was* tragic.

James pushed away his empty plate. "So, Radio Waves might get signed by an independent label. We could have a CD out by this time next year."

I was impressed. Immediately I envisioned myself the girlfriend of a rock star. I could go backstage, ride in limos, get free T-shirts. "Oh, yeah? Will you give me a private listening of your album?" I batted my eyelashes and gave James a big smile.

There. I'd actually managed to flirt. It hadn't been easy, and I'd felt pretty silly, but I was still alive. Maybe by the time James's CD was released, I'd be an expert.

He reached under the table and patted my knee. "Anytime, Delia. Anytime."

*　　　*　　　*

It was about eleven o'clock when James pulled up in front of my house. Nervous, I reached for the Jeep's door handle immediately. But James put a hand on my arm and pulled me back.

"You're funny, Delia," he whispered. Funny? That wasn't the adjective I'd been hoping for. "I could definitely get used to having you around."

Then he leaned forward and kissed me. At first all I could think was, "Oh, my gosh, I'm actually kissing *James Sutton*." But then I relaxed a little, concentrating on his warm, soft lips. I was glad we were sitting, because my knees felt wobbly, and I probably would have lost my balance if I'd been standing.

I kissed him back, trying not to think about the fact that my palms were sweating and my breath probably smelled like pepperoni. When he pulled away, I felt shaky and disoriented. "Sweet dreams, Delia," he murmured.

As I walked up the path to my house, I realized that "sweet dreams" was what Cain always said to me. Somehow the expression sounded a whole lot different coming from a guy who'd just kissed me on the lips. . . .

Sunday morning I went over to the Johnsons'. A few days a week I baby-sat their ten-year-old daughter, Nina. When I arrived at the house Nina was in the front yard practicing dance moves. Ever since she'd found out I taught dance, she'd insisted that dance was her number-one priority. Her number-two priority was talking about the boys at Lincoln Elementary.

"Hey, Nina," I called. "How are you coming with that new combo I taught you on Thursday?" I walked onto the lawn and flopped on the grass. I'd been up most of the night thinking about my date with James, and sleep deprivation was taking its toll.

"Great! Do you want to see me do it with music?" She was hopping up and down, waiting for my answer.

"I'd love to. Why don't you get your portable tape player? I'll wait here." I closed my eyes against the sun, glad it was still warm enough to be outside.

A minute later Nina walked back out with her parents, tape player in tow. As they shouted last-minute instructions to me, Nina rewound the tape I'd made for her.

We'd gone over her routine about fifteen times when Cain pulled up to the house. He loved visiting me at the Johnsons', because Nina worshiped the ground he walked on.

Nina stopped midstep and ran over to Cain. "Do you want to see my new dance, Cain?" she asked.

He walked over to the front steps and sat down. "Of course I do. You don't think I came here to see Delia, do you?"

Nina giggled and went over to rewind her tape yet again. I sat down next to Cain, relieved. Sometimes ten-year-old girls had more energy than I could handle.

"So, how was the big date last night?" Cain asked as we watched Nina leap happily across the lawn.

"Amazing." I wondered if Cain could tell by looking at me that James had kissed me the night before. I still remembered the gentle touch of his lips on mine.

"Are you sure you're not saying that just because you want to win our bet?" He looked at me with raised eyebrows.

"I'll have you know that our stupid bet is the last thing on my mind right now." It was a lie, but I was sick of Cain second-guessing me all the time.

"You didn't find Sutton the least bit boring?" Cain clapped as Nina finished her dance and curtsied. "Encore!" he shouted.

I signaled Nina to start from the beginning, then turned to Cain. "For your information, Radio Waves is about to get signed by a record label," I said huffily.

Cain snorted. "First of all, James has been saying that for over a year. Those guys have as much chance of making it in the music business as *I* do. Second of all, you didn't answer the question. Was he boring?"

"He's fascinating. More important, he finds *me* fascinating."

"I don't doubt that," Cain said. "After going out with Tanya Reed, you must seem like a rocket scientist."

"Thanks for the backhanded compliment." Cain was starting to irritate me. Despite our bet, I'd thought he would be happy that I'd found romance. On Labor Day, he'd acted as though my finding a boyfriend was the most important thing in the world to him.

"I'm sorry. Really. Just tell me one thing."

"What?" I asked, sighing heavily.

"How many times did he check his hair in the mirror?"

I had to laugh. James was pretty vain. I'd even noticed him trying to look at his reflection in the empty pizza pan.

Cain started imitating James preening in front of a full-length mirror, and we both lost it. By the time Nina finished her dance, she thought there was something wrong with us.

I walked Cain to his car, leaving Nina to pick up her stuff so that we could go inside and make lunch. I knew she was disappointed that Cain was leaving—she loved showing off for him.

"Seriously, how much do you like James?" Cain asked. He opened his car door and looked at me.

I thought about it for a minute. I'd never guessed that a guy like James Sutton would give me the time of day, much less possibly become my boyfriend. I'd have to be crazy to pass up an opportunity with him. Even if he ended up breaking my heart, I had to go for it. "I like him a ton," I said finally. "He might be the guy for me."

Cain shook his head. "Well, don't get out the razor for my head yet. A lot can happen between now and the Winter Ball. A whole lot."

Cain peeled out of the driveway. As I watched his car disappear around the corner, I had the distinct feeling that my best friend was up to something. Then again, when wasn't he?

Chapter Six

Cain

Tuesday, October 24
after school

I can't get my mind off Delia and James.
For the past two days I've seen them flirting.
A couple of times I even saw them holding
hands. It was weird to see Delia acting so
goofy. She seemed like a whole new person,
and I'm not sure I liked it. When I told her
back in September that she should fall in
love, I didn't know she'd do it so fast.

Sure, James is a good-looking guy—if
you like the pretty-boy type. And he is definitely popular. But his personality leaves a lot
to be desired. For one thing, I've never seen
Delia laugh when she's with him. When
she's with me she can't stop laughing.

Rebecca was away with her parents last
weekend, but we've got a definite date set

for Saturday. And if it doesn't go the way I
hope, I'll really be in trouble. . . .

There was no doubt I was getting nervous about
losing the bet. If I lost, I'd look like a total idiot, and
Delia would never, ever let me forget it. I'd also
have to put up with Andrew giving me a hard time
for about the next fifty years. And then there was
the tiny matter of falling in love. I was sick of being
alone, or just dating random girls. I wanted more
than just a good time.

I was definitely ready to take things with
Rebecca to another level. I already thought she was
one of the most beautiful women I'd ever seen. And
she was smart. Not to mention sophisticated. And
sexy. Okay, she was perfect.

I didn't know why I was so anxious when I
pulled up to her house on Saturday afternoon. Was
it because I'd found a girl I could really care about,
and now I was paralyzed by a fear of rejection? Or
had I just gotten rusty?

Anyway, I'd cleaned my car, inside and out, which
was a first for me. In the backseat I had a picnic basket
filled with sandwiches, chips, brownies, and soda
(supplied by my generous mother). As I walked up to
the Fosters' front door, I whistled cheerfully to myself. By the time I was through charming Rebecca,
Delia was going to have a run for her money.

A little blond kid answered the front door. He
was wearing a Power Rangers T-shirt and looked as
if he'd been playing in the dirt.

"Who are you?" he demanded, scowling at me.

"Cain Parson, sir. Are you the gentleman of the house?" I used my best salesman's voice, and he laughed. He opened the door wider and gestured for me to come inside.

"Are you my sister's boyfriend?" He was looking at me as if I were a lab specimen.

"I don't know. Maybe we should ask her."

"Jason, are you being a brat again?" Rebecca said, coming down the stairs. In a pair of black jeans and a tight green sweater, she looked as gorgeous as usual. Her hair was in a loose bun, but several tendrils had escaped, framing her face.

"No!" Jason answered, taking a step back.

"Get out of here. Go back to your mud puddle."

Jason raced up to Rebecca, stepped on her foot, then hightailed it down a long hallway.

"Cute kid," I said. "And his older sister is even cuter."

Rebecca gave me a quick kiss on the cheek. "He's a monster. Why can't children be born full-grown?" Apparently Rebecca wasn't too fond of children.

"That might be a little hard on mothers."

"Speaking of which, let's leave before my mom comes out to meet you. If she gets her claws in, she'll end up convincing you that your heart's desire is to sit in the kitchen and drink coffee with her." Rebecca picked up a faded jean jacket and threw it over her shoulder.

Once we started driving, Rebecca tried to find something good on the radio. "How many easy-listening stations does this town have? This stuff would be banned in Manhattan."

"There's a good jazz station," I said, changing the dial.

She shrugged. "All right. That's cool."

At a red light I turned to look at her. "Are you psyched for some picnic food?"

"Sure. As long as I don't have to eat any ants." She unbuckled her seat belt and slid a little closer to me. "Just where are we going?"

"Gambler's Pond," I said proudly. Usually I didn't take my dates there, but since Rebecca was special I wanted to share it with her.

"Sounds like something out of a Kenny Rogers song."

I laughed. Delia had said the same thing the first time we'd gone to the pond together. "Believe me, it's beautiful."

"As beautiful as Central Park?"

"Well, there are no carriage rides. But I guarantee that the pond is sewage-free." I put my right arm around her shoulder. It was going to be a great day.

"I guess I'll have to take my chances."

I turned off on the dirt road that led to the pond. "So, how are you adjusting to life at Jefferson?"

"It's okay. I've been buttering up some of the cheerleaders, so I should get on the squad next season. And from what I've seen of the student government, I think I'll have a good shot at president."

"Wow. You're pretty ambitious." Somehow

Rebecca had never struck me as a school-politics kind of a person.

"I like to leave my mark. And think about how good it'll look on my college applications."

"I think I see the New Yorker in you emerging." I stopped the car at the edge of the field next to Gambler's Pond. Even though it was a sunny, warm fall day, we were the only people there.

"This place *is* beautiful," Rebecca said, as if she'd secretly expected me to take her to a dump.

"Ms. Foster, may I present Gambler's Pond?"

She giggled and got out of the car. I grabbed the picnic basket and blanket, jogging to catch up with her.

"How cozy," Rebecca said as I walked up beside her.

"Yep. Just you, me, and the sun," I said. We each took a side of the blanket, and it billowed in the wind.

I anchored the four corners with rocks, then sat down. Leaning back on my elbows, I patted the spot next to me. "Madam, your table awaits."

Rebecca knelt beside me, opening up the picnic basket. "Ooh. Peanut butter and jelly."

"I tried to get caviar, but the A and P was fresh out."

"Caviar is a *bit* much for lunch. Peanut butter and jelly will be fine." She started taking food out of the basket. She looked so comfortable, it felt as if we'd been going on picnics together for years.

"Maybe we should bring Jason out here sometime," I said. "Think of all the awesome mud pies he could make."

Rebecca looked at me as if I'd just proposed we go on a wild killing spree. "Maybe not," she said shortly. "He's not exactly my idea of a great date."

I opened a can of soda and poured it into the plastic champagne glasses I'd brought. "How about a toast?" I asked.

She grinned. "As long as it doesn't involve my little brother, I'm all ears."

Around us, scarlet and yellow leaves drifted quietly to the ground. The pond was a clear blue, and the sun glinted off the water as if it were sprinkled with diamonds. All we needed was a guy with a violin, and Gambler's Pond would have been the most romantic place on earth.

I raised my glass. "To Gambler's Pond. And, in the words of John Denver, to sunshine on your shoulders."

"To us, and my new life in hometown America." Rebecca clinked her glass against mine, gazing at me from beneath her long eyelashes.

I set down my soda and moved closer to Rebecca. Our lips met, and I kissed her softly. Right away I felt a spark. Rebecca's lips tasted even better than they looked. My pulse began to race as I shifted my weight so that we were closer together on the blanket. As our kiss deepened I wished Delia were there to see it. She was going to have to eat my dust in the love department. Then Rebecca ran her fingers through my hair, and I didn't think about anything at all.

*   *   *

"It was great. I asked Rebecca to homecoming," I said to Andrew. We'd just finished an intense game of one-on-one at Jefferson's outdoor basketball court. The weather had gotten a little chilly, but I was sweating and slightly out of breath.

"Did she say yes?" He spun the basketball on the tip of his index finger—a trick he'd been trying to perfect for years.

"Dude, of course she said yes. Has a woman ever been able to resist my charms?"

"I can think of one." Andrew shoved the basketball into my stomach, and I groaned.

"Who?" I got up from the bench we were sitting on and dribbled the ball.

"Who do you think? Delia."

"Excuse me?" I caught the ball and stood motionless.

"Delia Byrne. The girl you've been mooning over forever. She's never fallen prey to your particular brand of manliness."

"Delia and I are *friends*. Look it up in the dictionary."

"Why don't you look up *denial* in the dictionary, man? You've got a bad case."

"I thought we were talking about Rebecca." We both picked up our backpacks and started walking toward the parking lot.

"We were. To tell you the truth, I don't understand why you're so desperate for a girlfriend. The dance is weeks away. Maybe you'll find someone better."

69

I shook my head. Andrew's total lack of sensitivity never ceased to astonish me. Even as a guy, I found the way he viewed girls offensive. "See, Andrew, there's this really cool stuff in life. Stuff called love, fulfillment, and happiness."

"And?" He stopped in his tracks, staring at me.

"And what?"

"You think you're going to find all that with Rebecca?" Andrew took the basketball. He spun it on his finger again.

"Sure. Why not?"

Andrew threw up his hands in surrender. "I just don't see how you can say you love some girl you've known for just a couple of months."

"Listen, I'm looking for something real. I don't see anything wrong with that." I started walking again, and Andrew followed me.

"Well, I like playing the field. Girls equal one giant headache, if you ask me."

"I didn't ask you."

"You should have. Rebecca's just looking for fun, man. She's not the kind of girl you want to fall in love with."

"I'll take that under advisement. Now, can I have my basketball?"

"Take the basketball," he said, handing it over. "And take it from me, you're heading for trouble."

I gave Andrew a not-so-soft punch in the arm. What did he know about women, anyway?

Chapter Seven

Delia

Wednesday, November 1
10:00 P.M.

James asked me to the homecoming dance yesterday! We were at Caroline Sung's Halloween party (I was a witch, he was a pirate), and he asked me in this blacklight room she'd set up. Earlier in the night, he'd been bugging me a little with all his talk about what he and Tanya did for Halloween last year (a haunted hayride, if you must know). I was also in a bad mood because Cain hadn't come to the party. He and Rebecca had gone to some football player's house instead.

But the important thing was that James asked me to the dance. Homecoming will be my first school dance with an official boyfriend. Does this mean we're in love?

*P.S. I can't wait to tell Cain my news. I
feel like we haven't talked in years.*

Winter was coming to Jefferson High. Everyone
was donning new sweaters and talking about how
they could see their breath in the cold air outside.
At night, I closed the windows in my room and
considered plugging in my electric blanket. When I
gave Nina Johnson her dance lessons, our stage was
the rec room in her basement instead of the front
yard. Ellen Frazier had decided it was time to start
wearing her Miracle Bra.

Despite my continued insistence that the whole
concept of high-school dances was immature and
stupid, I couldn't wait to walk in with James's arm
around me. I pictured a small corsage of red roses
pinned to my dress; rhinestone earrings would dan-
gle just above my exposed shoulders; my ankles
would be slim and provocative in the straps of my
high-heeled evening sandals.

Unfortunately, Radio Waves was playing at the
dance, so I wouldn't get to spend much actual time
with James. But I comforted myself with the
knowledge that every other girl in the gym would
be jealous that *I* was with the sexy lead singer.

Friday afternoon Ellen and I were in Duval's
shopping for dresses. She had agreed to go to the
dance with one of James's friends, although she
wasn't crazy about the idea.

"How about this one?" Ellen asked me. She giggled and held up a pink taffeta dress with a balloon

skirt. Around the shoulders were feathers of some kind. The dress was hideous.

"If I wore that getup, all you'd have to do is wrap me in a bad comic and I'd look like a piece of Bazooka bubble gum." I went over to another rack and pulled out a short black dress. It had a beaded bolero jacket, and it was absolutely perfect.

Ellen picked out a green silk sheath, and we headed for the dressing room. "So, I guess Cain and that Rebecca girl are getting pretty serious," Ellen said. She was pulling off her sweater, so her voice was slightly muffled, but I got it.

I started untying my black work boots. "They're going to homecoming together, if that's what you mean." I yanked off my boots, then my thick black socks—they wouldn't have looked great with a cocktail dress.

Ellen turned around so I could zip up the green dress. I could tell that "nature's helper," as she liked to call her bra, was going to do wonders for the dress. "Yeah, I knew they were going to the dance. I mean, Cain asked her a while ago. But that bracelet he gave her looks pretty expensive. Andrew Rice told me that Cain blew a big chunk of his summer bonus on it."

My hands stopped midzip. "What in the *world* are you talking about? What bracelet?"

In the mirror, I saw Ellen raise her eyebrows. "You don't know about it?"

I shook my head, trying to look nonchalant. "No, I guess he forgot to mention it. No big deal."

73

"Well, it's gold, and there's an opal on it. Opal's her birthstone. I saw the bracelet when we were both in the bathroom yesterday. The way she was holding up her wrist, I'd have to have been blind not to notice it."

I tried to look as if I had no interest in what Ellen was describing. "Hmm. I didn't know Cain was the kind of guy who'd do something as hokey as buying a girl her birthstone. There's something so sixties about that."

"I'm sure he'll tell you all about the bracelet. He probably hasn't had a chance yet." Ellen stood on her tiptoes, trying to discern what the dress would look like with pumps.

"Oh, yeah, I'm sure it probably just slipped his mind."

Inside I was furious. How could Cain have neglected to tell something as important as this to his best friend? And he'd obviously told Andrew about the gift—maybe he'd even *consulted* Andrew about what he should buy. Cain never got presents for his girlfriends—especially not expensive jewelry. The only thing he'd ever gotten *me* was a goldfish (which died after three days).

Maybe Cain really was in love with Rebecca. If so, then our bet would be a draw. Because I was almost positive that I was in love with James. But was Cain going to abandon me now that he'd found someone better? In the past, our friendship had always come first. He'd tell me anything and everything about his life—and the tell-all attitude

74

included his love life. Now it seemed as if he didn't need me at all. Maybe I'd said good-bye to my best friend. It was a depressing thought, to say the least.

Ellen turned around in front of the three-way mirror, smoothing the green silk over her chest. She looked like a size 34B at least. "Well, I think Cain's going out with Rebecca Foster is a complete waste of a great guy. She is the absolute worst."

"Why's that?" I had to admit to myself that I didn't have very warm feelings toward Rebecca. Every time I met her it was as if I'd just walked into a meat locker. But I was used to getting the cold shoulder from Cain's girlfriends—it didn't bother me at all. In fact, I kind of got a kick out of it. Still, I was surprised that Ellen seemed to have such a negative opinion of Cain's latest conquest.

"Ugh. The girl is a total social climber. I heard her bragging about Cain in the women's room. She went on and on about how good he looked, but she didn't say a word about his awesome personality." Ellen unzipped her dress and stepped out of it.

"Really?" I was still studying myself in the mirror. Somehow the black dress had lost its appeal. I had a heavy feeling in my stomach, and all of a sudden shopping was the last activity I was in the mood for.

"Then I heard her tell Amanda Wright that Cain was her ticket to popularity. Since everybody knows who he is, they'll automatically know who she is. She said that by the time she was a senior, she'd be captain of the cheerleading squad and going out with the quarterback. How shallow can you get?"

I hung up the black dress and the bolero jacket. "You're not jealous of Rebecca, are you? I mean, I know you've got a crush on Cain, but he's not great boyfriend material—he's way too fickle. Believe me, you're better off his friend."

Ellen frowned. "Delia, I am *not* jealous. Are you?"

"Don't make me laugh," I said indignantly. "I'd never go out with Cain. I've told you that at least a thousand times."

"I know that's what you *say*." Ellen pulled on her jeans and reached for her shoes. "But you never tell me exactly why you don't want to go out with him."

I sighed. "For one thing, I'm into James. Even if I wasn't, Cain and I would never be right for each other."

"Expand," Ellen said, arching an eyebrow at me.

"He's like a brother, he can't commit, he's arrogant, we have different taste in ice cream, we get into stupid fights about who gets to handle the remote control, we . . ."

I knew I was babbling, but Ellen's probing questions were starting to get to me. Talking about Cain in such a personal way made me distinctly uncomfortable.

Ellen laughed. "Well, I can see that you two were a match made in hell. I'll drop the subject. I know you hate talking about Cain."

"Thank you. Now, let's get out of here. My dream dress isn't on any of these racks."

As we walked out of Duval's I tried to ignore the gnawing feeling in the pit of my stomach. I still couldn't believe that Cain hadn't told me about buying

Rebecca a fancy bracelet. As soon as I got home I was going to call him. He had a lot of explaining to do.

I twisted the telephone cord around my finger as I waited for one of the Parsons to answer. On the third ring, I heard Mrs. Parson's warm voice.

"Hi, Mrs. Parson. May I speak with Cain?" I kicked off my boots and lay back on my bed.

"Delia! It's so good to hear your voice. I feel like I haven't seen you in so long."

"Well, I've been pretty busy. I guess Cain has been, too." Mrs. Parson was one of my favorite people in the world. She was almost like a second mother.

"Deels?" Cain had picked up another phone, and Mrs. Parson hung up hers.

"Hey." For some reason my heart started racing. All of a sudden, Cain sounded like a stranger.

"What're you up to tonight?" I could hear him eating something—from the crunching sound, I figured he was probably munching on corn chips. He went through almost a bag a day.

"I have a date with James." I took the phone over to my closet. James was picking me up in half an hour, and I still had no idea what I was going to wear.

"Looks like our bet might become moot." His voice sounded a little tired, as if he didn't really want to be talking to me.

"So I hear," I responded, unable to keep the bitter tone out of my voice.

"What's that supposed to mean?" I could tell he was irritated, but I really didn't care.

"You and Rebecca are getting pretty close. Everyone's talking about the extravagant bracelet you found it necessary to buy her."

"It was her birthday. So what?"

"Why didn't you tell me you were so in love with her that you were willing to blow your summer bonus? I'm not important enough for you to fill me in about your life?" I was getting angrier and angrier. Cain could have at least asked me to help select the gift. I had better taste than he did.

"Excuse me for even *having* a life. I thought you were too busy kissing James Suckface in the halls to care what *I* was doing." Now Cain was mad, too, and I could tell our conversation was headed downhill.

"Ha! Your lips are glued to Rebecca's. I'm starting to think you two are Siamese twins."

Abruptly Cain stopped his crunching. "I think you're worried that I'm going to win the bet. You're getting sick of that sorry excuse for a boyfriend, and you know he's not going to last until the Winter Ball."

I pulled out a pair of knit pants and a turtleneck sweater. Then I slammed shut my closet door. "I am totally, completely in love with James Sutton. You, on the other hand, wouldn't know love if it knocked you on the head. All you care about is a pretty face."

With the help of my free hand I struggled out of my jeans. Time was ticking away, and I still hadn't changed my clothes. I was using all of my self-control not to hang up on Cain.

"Delia, you don't know a thing about me. Obviously you've spent the last three years in a fog."

"Obviously," I responded sarcastically. "Now if you'll excuse me, I have to finish getting ready for my date. Have a wonderful life."

"Same to you." His voice was barely audible.

"Good-bye." I set down the receiver with a violent bang. I was on the verge of tears, and James was going to be outside honking in less than ten minutes.

As furious as I was with Cain, I couldn't believe our conversation had ended so badly. We'd never been so mean to each other, and I wasn't sure that we could get past the ugliness.

I tried to get excited about seeing James, but tears were working their way down my cheeks. My face in the mirror was pale, my eyes red. I might have been in love, but I looked like I'd just lost my best friend.

"Do you know how beautiful you look tonight?" James asked, pulling me close.

I leaned my head against his chest, listening to his rapid heartbeat. "You're not so bad yourself."

We'd gone out for a huge Italian dinner, and now we were standing at my front door. James had been so attentive during our date, I'd felt like a princess.

"Delia, I'm so glad we found each other. I was really bummed out at the beginning of the year. When Tanya left, I thought I'd be alone for the rest of my life. And then I walked into creative writing, and there you were."

"Sounds like fate to me." I looked into James's hazel eyes, wanting to lose myself in his sensuous gaze. I was truly living out a fairy tale.

"Me too." James's mouth was so close to mine that I felt, rather than heard, his words. I wound my arms around his neck, pulling him even closer. He brought one hand up to my face, stroking my cheek as if it were satin. I ran my fingertip lightly over the tender skin at the back of his neck and felt him shiver in my arms.

For a moment we just stared at each other. Then James kissed me, parting my lips with his. I felt tingles all over my body, but a weird feeling of confusion mixed with bliss washed over me. I had what I wanted, but there was this haunting sense of a major letdown. Why?

Ignoring my brain, I pressed closer, shutting my eyes against the dim glow of the light shining over our front door.

I don't know how long we stood together, locked in an embrace unlike any I'd ever shared. But when we finally stepped back from each other, we were both breathless.

At that moment the light above the door flashed on and off several times. Apparently my mother knew I was standing outside and felt that my world had been rocked enough for one evening. I gave an embarrassed laugh.

James smiled, smoothing my hair behind my ears. He leaned forward to give a quick peck on my forehead, then tilted his head toward my ear. "I'll sing a song just for you at the dance," he whispered.

I slipped inside the house, noticing that my mother had discreetly left the front hallway.

Stepping over to the living room window, I pushed back the white gauzy curtain. James had gotten into his Jeep, and his face was now obscured by shadows. I heard the faint sound of whistling and let the curtain drop back in place.

As I tiptoed upstairs a part of me felt as if I were floating on cloud nine. I'd achieved my senior-year goal. It wasn't even homecoming, and I'd fallen in love for the first time in my life. Who would have guessed that cynical Delia Byrne was capable of evoking the light I'd seen in James's eyes that night? It really was as if a miracle had occurred.

But another part of me felt as if I'd been run over by a car. Although I could call Ellen and give her a detailed account of my passionate night with James, Cain's door was closed to me. And if I couldn't share the events of my life with the person I cared about most in the world, it was almost as if they hadn't happened at all.

Chapter Eight

Cain

BY THE TIME I got to physics class Monday morning, I was feeling pretty anxious about seeing Delia. We hadn't spoken since our catastrophic phone conversation on Saturday night, and I still wasn't sure exactly what we'd gotten into such a huge fight about. One second we'd been talking like sane human beings, and the next we'd been shouting at each other as if we were enemies at war. The experience had been completely unsettling, and I hadn't been able to get it off my mind since.

Delia walked into class after I did, and she sat down at the desk directly next to mine. Since there were several empty desks, I took her gesture as a sign that she wanted to make up with me.

Once Ms. Gordon launched into a lecture about throwing pennies off the Empire State Building, I tore out a piece of notebook paper. "TRUCE?" I wrote in big block letters. (I was willing to make the first move, but I wasn't going to go so far as to apologize.)

For the last fifteen minutes Delia had been making a big show of keeping her face averted from mine. Now I poked her in the arm with my pencil, holding up the piece of paper. She whipped her head around. When she saw my note, she gave me a little smile. I reached out and gave her hair a pull, then set down the note. All of a sudden I felt as if a two-ton weight had been lifted from my shoulders.

When the bell rang, Delia got up, took a couple of steps over toward me, and put her hands on my shoulders. "Friends?" she said.

I nodded, squeezing one of her hands. "Always."

When we got out of the classroom, I turned to her. "How about going to Winstead's after school? We can have some nachos and remind ourselves that we don't hate each other."

"Excellent idea, Parson. I'll meet you at three o'clock."

Rebecca was waiting for me in the hallway. The bracelet I'd given her gleamed against her wrist. I glanced over at Delia, who had a huge smile plastered on her face.

"Hi, guys," Rebecca said, beaming at me.

"Hey, Rebecca," Delia said. "That's a beautiful bracelet." Delia sounded as if she were talking to her best friend, and I was relieved that she was making an attempt to be nice to Rebecca.

Rebecca held up her wrist. "Thanks, Delia. Sugar Cain gave it to me. Isn't he sweet?" She clasped my hand and stepped closer.

I saw Delia roll her eyes. Her deep brown eyes were intense, but I couldn't tell exactly what she was thinking. "As sweet as sugar," Delia agreed. "See you lovebirds later."

As Delia walked quickly down the hall Rebecca reached up and kissed me on the cheek. "Guess what?" she asked.

"What?" I still had one eye on Delia, who was standing with James next to the fire exit. She was laughing, and it was hard to believe that she was the same girl who'd gotten so angry on Saturday night.

"I talked to Carrie Starks. And we decided that she and Patrick would double with you and me at the dance Saturday night."

I frowned, remembering how obnoxious Patrick Mayor usually was at school dances. He was not someone I was dying to associate myself with. And since he'd started dating Carrie Starks, the two of them had engaged in more public displays of affection than I cared to think about. There was something incredibly distasteful about watching a beefy football player paw his girlfriend in broad daylight. But Rebecca didn't seem to notice that I wasn't thrilled.

"Won't it be great?" she said. "We'll all have such an awesome time together. And if I become good friends with Carrie, then I'll be a shoo-in for the cheerleading squad."

If she really wanted to go to the dance with Patrick and Carrie, what did I care? After all, the better the mood she was in, the more romantic she'd feel. And dances were meant for romance.

"That'll be a lot of fun," I said, throwing my arm around her. "I'll drive."

We separated at the door of Rebecca's next class, and I ran up the stairs to Jefferson's library, taking the steps two at time. Andrew and I were doing an oral report for history together, and we both had second-period study hall.

I found him at a table in the middle of the library with about twenty thick books spread out around him. He had a pencil in his mouth, and he looked much more like a serious student than he really was.

"What's up, Rice?" I said, pulling up a chair.

"Shh. This is a library." Andrew put a finger over his lips, indicating that I should be quiet.

I leaned close so that he could hear me whisper. "What's with the Boy Scout routine?" I asked, glancing around to see if the principal was standing guard.

Andrew pointed to a girl behind the checkout desk of the library. Lots of juniors got stuck with library duty, but I'd never seen Andrew so in awe of the position. The girl had long brown hair and was wearing a button-down oxford-cloth shirt. He turned to me and said, "I promised Rachel we'd be quiet."

I raised my eyebrows. Had aliens stolen Andrew and replaced his body with a clone? I'd never seen him worry about a promise to a library attendant before. "So what?"

"She's an awesome girl. Let's show her some respect," Andrew whispered, shifting his eyes back to where Rachel was punching something into a computer.

I reached out to feel his forehead. "Do you have a fever? Or have you lost your mind?"

He swatted my hand away. "We should get to work. Rachel was nice enough to find us these books. Let's use them."

I opened the book closest to me and started thumbing through the pages. After a few minutes I lifted my head to ask Andrew how he wanted to divide up the work. He was staring at Rachel, and his mouth was hanging open. I waved my hand up and down in front of his eyes, trying to get his attention.

As I watched a blush rise to his cheeks, I was struck with a mind-blowing thought. Whether or not he knew it, renegade Andrew had fallen for the girl who worked in the library.

"Her name is Rachel," I said to Delia, holding open Winstead's glass door for her. "She works in the library."

Winstead's was one of a kind. It had everything from hamburgers to burritos, although most of the food tasted pretty much the same. The tables were well-worn, and there was an old jukebox in one corner. I think Delia and I had spent half our waking lives in the place, especially before we got our driver's licenses. Winstead's was a popular hangout for underclassmen, because it was only a bike ride away from where most people lived.

"Rachel Hall?" Delia asked, making a beeline to

our favorite table. It was right next to the jukebox; Delia tended to dominate the music selection whenever we were in the place.

"I guess so. Andrew just called her Rachel. And he had this totally goofy expression on his face whenever her name passed his lips." I hung both of our jackets on a peg next to the table, then fell into my seat—it had been a long day.

"Very interesting. Somehow I don't think Rachel was on Andrew's senior wish list."

Delia opened a menu between us, and I craned my neck so I could read the words upside down.

"Well, I think he really has a thing for her."

"I wonder if she'd be into him," Delia said, pushing the menu toward me. "Do you want to split some nachos?"

"I've been dreaming about nachos since tuna surprise at lunch," I said. "Anyway, they don't really seem like each other's type. But love works in mysterious ways."

"If anyone knows that, it's us," Delia agreed. She gave our order to the waitress. Then she leaned over to put a dollar in the jukebox.

"True. I mean, less than three months ago, we thought we'd never fall in love. Now here we are." I grinned at Delia, and she smiled back.

The waitress returned with our order almost immediately. Basically, the nachos consisted of store-bought chips covered with melted cheese-food spread. On the side of the plate was a pile of jalapeços. That said, Winstead's nachos were possibly my all-time favorite food.

Delia picked up a soggy chip and stuffed it into her mouth whole. "You know, Cain, I have to admit something to you."

"What's that?" I asked.

"I'm really glad you made me agree to that stupid bet. I don't know if I would have been sending love signals to James if I hadn't had the threat of a bleached-blond hairdo hanging over my head."

"Well, I'm happy for you in your new role as girl-in-love, but I still think James is a loser." I ate another nacho, savoring the taste of melted cheese.

"You're just saying that because you want to win the bet. Can't you even be satisfied with a tie?"

I knew she wasn't going to take any advice from me, but I couldn't help offering an opinion. It was in my nature. "I am *not* just saying that to win the bet. I'm totally serious."

"What if I said I didn't think Rebecca was good enough for you?" One of the songs Delia had selected on the jukebox came on, and she started swaying back and forth in time to it.

"I'd tell you to mind your own business," I responded.

"Exactly."

"So you're telling me to mind my own business."

"That's right, Sherlock."

I waved my napkin as a white flag. "You've got a deal."

She nodded. "I thought you'd see things my way."

Delia pushed away the plate of nachos and downed her glass of water in one long gulp. Watching her, I laughed. She really was one in a million.

November 11, homecoming Saturday, was cold and sunny. Friday afternoon I'd gotten all of my dance preparations out of the way: my mother had helped me pick out a red rose corsage for Rebecca, I'd picked up my one and only suit from the dry cleaners, and I'd even washed my car. I was set.

Since Patrick was on the football team and Carrie was a cheerleader, Rebecca and I were going alone to the afternoon Raiders game. Then we'd both go home and change, and I'd swing by to get everyone around nine o'clock. I still wasn't dying to double with Patrick and Carrie, but I'd resigned myself to their unstimulating company.

When we got to the game, Rebecca pulled me over to the section of the bleachers that was right in front of the cheerleaders.

"Let's sit here," she said. "So we can see all of our friends." She waved to Carrie, who shook a red pom-pom at us.

I saw Andrew out of the corner of my eye. He was alone, so I gestured for him to come sit with us. The woebegone expression on his face was decidedly uncharacteristic.

Rebecca stood up and gave him a hug as he sat down. "Hey, Andy, how are you?"

He scratched his head and rubbed at the light

stubble on his cheeks. "To tell you the truth, I've been better."

Rebecca didn't seem to have heard his answer. "So, who're you taking to the dance?"

Andrew shook his head. "I'm not going."

"I thought you were going to ask Rachel Hall," I said. He'd been building up his nerve for two days, and he'd sworn that he was going to ask her after school on Friday.

"I decided it would be an insult. You can't ask a girl to homecoming the day before the dance. It would look like you didn't think she could get a date."

"Rachel Hall?" Rebecca said, wrinkling her nose. "You mean that blah-looking girl in the library?"

I nudged Rebecca in the ribs. She was beautiful and intelligent, but diplomacy wasn't her strong point. "I think she's really pretty," I said.

Andrew shrugged. "Maybe Rebecca's right. What do I have in common with a chick who works in the library, anyway?"

"You don't want to go out with her," Rebecca said firmly. "I'm positive you could get someone much more popular."

"Delia really likes Rachel," I said. "She was in her English class last year, and they used to talk about books all the time." I glanced at Rebecca, trying to tell her with my eyes to lay off Andrew. Rachel was the first girl I'd ever seen him have a major thing for, and I didn't want Rebecca to thwart him.

"Well, Delia's liking her doesn't say much. She doesn't exactly have her finger on the pulse of

Jefferson High." Rebecca's voice sounded sweet, but her words made my stomach churn.

"What does that mean?" I'd almost forgotten that Andrew was sitting next to us. Rebecca had my full attention.

"Well, I doubt Delia would make the who's who of popular seniors. She's nice, but . . ." Rebecca let her voice trail off, as if she'd said everything there was to say about Delia.

"But what? Deels doesn't hang out with all those people because she's got better things to do with her time. Like dance. And write. And hang out with me."

I knew I was being cranky, but I couldn't help myself. If there was anything that made my blood boil, it was hearing something negative about Delia. *I* could talk for hours about how much she irritated me, but when anyone else opened their mouth, I felt a huge desire to punch something.

"Pardon me, Cain. I was just making a simple observation." Rebecca sounded hurt, and I immediately sensed that I'd come on too strong. After all, it was a free country. She could say whatever she wanted. Besides, Delia didn't need me fighting her battles.

"I'm sorry," I said contritely. "I guess I'm just a little big-brotherish when it comes to Byrne. Andrew knows what I mean, don't you?"

I looked to my left, expecting Andrew to break the tension with a joke. Unfortunately, he'd gotten up and left. I could see the back of his black leather jacket as he made his way to the concession stand.

"Never mind," Rebecca said, laying a hand on my

knee. "I'm sure we can find much more entertaining ways to amuse ourselves than talking about Delia."

I nodded mutely, putting my arm around her. "I second that motion. Let's talk about us."

As Rebecca launched into a speech about how much I was going to like her dress for the dance, I took a surreptitious glance around the stands.

To our right, and up several rows, Delia was sitting with James. They had a big plaid blanket around them, and I couldn't tell whether or not she and Suckface (as I always called him in my mind) were holding hands. Not that I cared. But from a purely anthropological standpoint, I always found it interesting to observe Delia behaving in ways that were contrary to her nature. In other words, I was curious.

Ellen Frazier was sitting behind James and Delia. I was certain that the guy next to her was her date for the dance, but there was about three feet of bench between them. Ellen had a contemptuous look on her face, and I couldn't help laughing. Delia had told me about Ellen's Miracle Bra, so I narrowed my eyes and took a closer look. As far as I could tell, she looked the same as she always had. But she was wearing a heavy sweater; I made a mental note to check her out at the dance.

My eyes traveled involuntarily back to Delia. I was desperate to know what was going on under that blanket. Just then she looked in my direction. Her eyes widened, then she averted her gaze. I felt the color rising to my cheeks. Had she thought I was staring at her?

Rebecca's voice cut into my thoughts. "My dad said I could stay out two hours later than normal curfew. Is that great or what?"

I moved closer on the bench and gave Rebecca as big a bear hug as I could, considering the fact that I was sitting down. "That's great. Just great."

"I know. Especially because the star of the basketball team is supposedly having an after-dance party. It's invitation only, but I'm sure we'll be on the list."

I groaned silently, tilting my face back in Delia's direction. Our eyes met briefly, and I saw her jump. The blanket slid from her lap, and I finally saw that she and Suckface were indeed holding hands.

I closed my eyes, wondering if she was finding true love as difficult to deal with as I was. Somehow I didn't think so.

Chapter Nine

Delia

HAVE YOU EVER noticed that all high-school dances have themes? There was never just a big party in the gym, with cool lights, a band, and some punch. There seems to be an unwritten law that students have to be subjected to the whim of some well-meaning decorations committee. For the homecoming dance, the committee had chosen "An Evening in Paris."

I had to admit that the gym looked pretty, in a Jefferson High sort of way. There were white lights strung up all over the walls, and even on the ceiling. The room was lined with tiny caf tables, complete with wrought-iron chairs and votive candles. On the walls were huge student-done paintings of famous Paris sights. And directly under the basketball hoop was a papier-mâché sculpture of the Eiffel Tower. It wasn't the ultimate Paris experience, but I had to give the committee credit. It must have taken them hours to string all those lights.

James and I had arrived at the dance early, since Radio Waves had to set up their equipment and do a sound check. Now the band was in full swing, although a lot of people hadn't arrived yet. At the moment I was dividing my time between watching James sing and watching other girls watch James sing. I loved the rapt expressions on their faces; their glazed eyes reminded me of my own.

"What do you think of gay Paree?" I heard Ellen say. She'd come up behind me, and I was thrilled to see her. As good as James looked onstage, I was tired of standing by myself.

"It's a sight to behold. But where's the Seine?"

Ellen laughed. "If enough cups of punch spill, there'll be a river running right through the middle of the gym."

"Hey, what happened to Sam?"

Ellen's date was James's friend Sam. They'd driven to the dance with us, but now Sam was nowhere in sight.

"He's hanging out in the parking lot with some of his buddies. I think we can definitely rule him out as Mr. Right."

"Well, you look beautiful. You should keep an eye out for other interesting prospects."

Ellen really did look incredible. We'd both gone back to Duval's and bought the dresses we'd tried on. Ellen looked every inch a prom queen, although I was still convinced that she didn't need the enhancement of her Miracle Bra.

"I did meet one guy. In fact, I see him standing alone next to the Eiffel Tower. I think I'll join him. Cultural sights are always so much more enjoyable when shared by a fellow traveler."

Once Ellen was gone, I felt like a wallflower. The gym had filled up with students, and it seemed as if I was the only person standing alone in the whole place. I was bored, and I was frustrated. Radio Waves would be performing for the rest of the night, and everyone else I knew was on the dance floor.

My new pumps were killing my feet, so I decided to seek refuge at one of the caf tables. From my vantage point in the little chair, I saw that Cain had come in with Rebecca, Patrick Mayor, and Carrie Starks. I could always feel Cain's presence in a room. Over the past few years I'd developed some kind of homing device that alerted me to his whereabouts. Sometimes I almost felt we had something like that twin ESP that people on talk shows were always talking about.

After watching Cain and Rebecca move onto the dance floor, I leaned my head against the wall and closed my eyes. I'd had a long day, and there were hours to go.

My eyes popped open when I heard James speaking into the microphone. "I'd like to dedicate this song to Delia Byrne," he said in his low, raspy voice. "She's my brown-eyed girl."

A hundred pairs of eyes were on me immediately. I stood up and gave James a little wave, feeling myself blush. I was sure my pulse rate had doubled.

I'd never had anyone sing to me before; the idea seemed the height of romance. Looking at James's smiling face, I shivered with pleasure. Radio Waves launched into their own version of "Brown-Eyed Girl" by Van Morrison. The tempo was slow and sultry, perfect for "A Paris Evening."

But even though I was listening to a song being played just for me, I was depressed. I hadn't been on the dance floor even once, and now I was going to have to stand on the sidelines and watch everyone else have fun.

"May I have this dance, little lady?"

I whipped around. Cain was beside me, his blue eyes twinkling. In his navy blue suit and paisley tie, he looked elegant and sophisticated. He'd had his dark hair trimmed. Basically, he looked like a *GQ* cover model.

"It would be my pleasure, sir," I responded, stepping into his arms.

Cain was scanning the floor, and I thought he was trying to keep an eye on Rebecca. I was wrong. "So Andrew never showed up," he commented.

"Rachel Hall isn't here, either. I checked."

Cain shook his head. "What a waste, huh? They're probably both sitting at home, totally miserable."

"Thank goodness that's not us," I said.

Cain pulled me a little closer. "Thank goodness," he agreed. Then we both fell silent.

Cain and I hadn't danced together much. He'd been to every school dance in the history of Jefferson High, but I'd only attended a few. And my usual pattern was that as soon as I arrived, I'd start figuring out a way to ditch my date and head for the hills. As I said before, I'd never been lucky in love.

"You look great, Deels," Cain said, looking into my eyes. We'd moved into the middle of the dance floor, and I was incredibly aware that his arms were wrapped tightly around me. But it wasn't as if he had a choice—we were dancing to a slow song, so he *had* to hold me close.

"Do you really think so?" I asked. Cain almost never gave me compliments; we were more into affectionate teasing.

He nodded. "Yep."

"Thanks. But why are you being so nice? It's unnerving."

I was aware of James's sexy voice singing in the background, but I was focusing all of my attention on Cain.

He laughed. "Am I being nice? Ignore me." He spun me around, then dipped me almost to the floor. The serious expression had completely left his face. "Hey, do you think that dress is tight enough? It looks like it's sewn on."

Now that was the Cain I knew. "Yeah? Well, let me ask *you* something," I said, giggling. "How many tubes of hair gel did you use tonight? Three, maybe four?"

We both broke out laughing. Then, as James picked up the speed of the song a bit, I started leading Cain in something that resembled a tango. We shot across the dance floor, forcing other couples to clear a path for us.

By the time the music slowed down again, we'd reached the other side of the gym. There wasn't much light, and we were left dancing in the shadows. Cain pulled me close again, and I found myself putting my arms around his neck.

All of a sudden I felt completely out of breath. I was acutely conscious of both the pulse in my neck having accelerated to a hundred beats a second and the firmness of Cain's muscles beneath my hands.

When I tilted my head to look into his face, I found Cain's mouth just millimeters from mine. Time seemed to stop, and I couldn't tear myself away from the piercing light in his eyes. *This is what other girls see,* I thought. *This is a Cain I've never known before.*

I moved my head closer to his, closing my eyes. I almost felt sick to my stomach, but I couldn't stop myself.

"May I cut in?" I heard a high-pitched voice hiss in my ear.

"Rebecca!" Cain said, abruptly stepping away from me. "I was just going to come find you."

"Well, here I am," she said, pointedly ignoring me.

"Here you are," I said, moving even farther away from Cain. "I'll catch you later, Parson."

I pushed my way through the couples on the dance floor, determined to locate Ellen. I was in dire need of some cynical banter about how stupid school dances were.

When I'd made it halfway across the room, I turned to sneak a glance at Cain. He was staring at me, but I was too far away to read the expression in his eyes. My breath caught in my throat, and I felt paralyzed.

At that moment Rebecca pulled Cain's head down for a kiss, and the spell was broken. I wasn't exactly sure what had just happened between Cain and me, but I hoped and prayed that whatever it was never happened again.

"What a rush," James said hours later. "I always love singing in front of a crowd."

It was almost one o'clock in the morning, and I'd called my mother an hour before to tell her that I was going to be late for curfew. The dance had ended, but James and the rest of Radio Waves had to stick around to pack up their equipment.

"You guys were great," I said, shoving a bunch of extension cords into a canvas bag. "Everybody loved you."

"What can I say? Rock and roll is in my blood." James picked up his guitar and sat down in one of the wrought-iron chairs. He played a twelve-bar blues riff, humming under his breath.

"So, how else can I help?" I asked, looking around the nearly empty stage. I was exhausted, and I had to get up early to baby-sit Nina.

James reached out and grabbed my hand, pulling me into the chair next to his. "I've got those I-don't-want-to-take-Delia-home blues," he sang, repeating the riff on his guitar.

I laughed. "Come on, Mick Jagger. My dad's going to send out the National Guard if I'm not home soon."

When we pulled up at my house, the ever-present

porch light was on. Through the curtains, I could make out the form of my mother waiting up for me on the couch.

James turned off the ignition and switched off the Jeep's headlights. He turned in his seat and reached over to put his hands on my hips. He pulled me close, kissing me with more intensity than he ever had before.

Sheltered by the dark night, I felt enveloped in a warm cocoon. Images of the football game, the dance, and even my mom waiting in the living room dropped away. I was only aware of lips, hands, and the quiet sound of our breathing.

Chills ran up and down my spine, and every nerve in my body tingled with excitement. "Cain," I whispered, feeling his soft hair beneath my fingertips.

In the next second my heart stopped. I opened my eyes, unable to believe what word had just passed my lips. With increasing alarm, I realized that I'd just called James by Cain's name. What was I thinking? Had he noticed?

I pulled my head back an inch and stared at James's face. In response he hugged me, squeezing my shoulders tightly. He obviously hadn't heard me utter Cain's name. A huge wave of relief washed over me. But I couldn't concentrate on James's kisses. Cain's name was echoing in my mind, the sound of it mocking me. Why had I said it? What was wrong with me?

I shook my head slightly, trying to clarify my thoughts. Forcing myself to think logically, I told myself that saying Cain's name didn't mean anything at all. I'd just seen Cain, and he was on my mind. That didn't take away from the fact that I was totally thrilled to be making out with James.

"I never want to stop kissing you," James said, gently holding my head between his hands.

"I love you," I whispered, burying my face against his shoulder.

I'd never said those words to a guy before (except Cain, but that was different), and I'd always imagined bells ringing and fireworks shooting into the sky when the time finally came. I didn't feel any of those things with James, but I figured that I'd been expecting too much. At that moment I was positive that I meant the words I'd said. James Sutton was my destiny. Period.

It wasn't until I'd turned off the light on my nightstand that I realized James hadn't said "I love you" back to me. But I was sure he would—soon.

"Did you dance all night?" Nina asked, pulling a carton of Ben and Jerry's ice cream from the freezer.

I got out two bowls and spoons. "No. James's band was playing, so I didn't really have anyone to dance with."

Nina sighed dramatically. "Dances are so romantic. I wish I could go to one."

Over the last couple of months, Nina had become interested in the whole concept of boys and dating. She asked me endless questions about both Cain and James, wanting to know the difference between a "boy who was a friend" and a boyfriend.

When I'd gotten to her house that morning, she'd been hopping up and down, dying to grill me about the dance. I wondered if I'd ever seen high-school dances through such rose-colored glasses. Observing Nina's sweet, happy face, I felt like a bitter old woman.

"Don't worry. You've got a hundred dances to look forward to. I bet every boy in your class will jump at the chance to take you to homecoming." I dished out two bowls of ice cream, setting one of them in front of Nina.

"Was Cain at the dance?" Since she and her friends had started getting boy-crazy, Nina had developed an even bigger crush on Cain.

"Yeah. He was there with his girlfriend, Rebecca."

Nina frowned—she didn't like the idea that Cain was going out with some girl she'd never seen before. "Well, did you dance with him, at least?"

"Yep. Once." I hoped Nina didn't notice my cheeks turning red. I could feel my face growing hot at the memory of the tension that had hovered between Cain and me during those few minutes of "Brown-Eyed Girl." It wasn't something I had any intention of discussing with Nina.

"Do you think Cain would want to take me to a dance?"

I laughed. "Isn't he a little old for you?"

Nina shrugged. "I'm mature for my age."

I put a huge spoonful of Chunky Monkey into my mouth. "I'll put in a good word for you," I said, grinning.

Nina ate quietly for a moment, then looked at me with a serious expression on her face. "Are you and Cain going to get married someday?"

I nearly choked on my ice cream. "No!" Nina and I had been over the fact that Cain and I were just friends a thousand times, but she refused to accept the notion that he wasn't my ideal man.

Nina looked at me thoughtfully. "Well, I think you should marry him. And I'll be your bridesmaid."

Experience had taught me that there was no use arguing with Nina, so I just shook my head and rolled my eyes. The little girl had a lot to learn about love.

Chapter Ten

Cain

*B*ASKING IN THE sun at Gambler's Pond, Rebecca and I lounged on a thick plaid blanket. I looked out at the water, thinking about how happy I was to be young and in love.

Hearing the tinkling sound of female laughter, I turned my head. But it wasn't Rebecca who was laughing. It was Delia. She was shielding her eyes from the light of the sun, and her tan, well-muscled legs were stretched out in front of her.

Without questioning her presence, I lay down with my head in her lap, smiling into her sparkling eyes. Slowly she bent down and brushed her lips across the sensitive skin next to my earlobe. Then her mouth moved to mine, and I reached upward, tangling my fingers in her wild mass of black hair. Hoisting myself into a sitting position, I increased the pressure of my lips. In the next second, we were *hugging, holding each other so tightly that I felt as if we were two halves of the same person. . . .*

In the middle of kissing Delia, I woke up. My heart was pounding, and beads of sweat were forming at my temples. My world felt as if it had been thrown completely off balance. What had just happened?

Of course, I'd dreamed about Delia lots of times. Everyone I knew had been featured in my sleep at one time or another. But I'd never dreamed that we were *kissing*. I felt like someone had slapped me in the face. *Rebecca* was the person I should be fantasizing about! She was my girlfriend, and I was in love with her. But that long kiss with Delia had felt so real, my lips ached just thinking about it.

The digital clock next to my bed read 12:15 P.M. A little chagrined that I'd slept so late, I stumbled into my bathroom to brush my teeth, pushing any thoughts of Delia out of my mind.

Everyone knew that dreams didn't mean anything. Just because I'd dreamed that I kissed Delia, it didn't mean that I actually wanted to kiss her. We'd shared what some people might call a romantic dance the night before, and having an innocent dream about her was entirely natural.

I splashed ice-cold water on my face, deciding that I would go out and find a pickup game of basketball. Some exercise was exactly what I needed. The dream about Delia had meant nothing. "Nothing at all," I said to my reflection in the mirror. "Zilch. Zero."

*   *   *

"Yo, Parson, how was the dance?" Andrew asked Monday morning.

We were in the library, meeting about our oral report again. Our topic was Egyptian pyramids. I was studying the historical background, and Andrew was working on the actual pyramids and the tombs inside.

"The band sucked, but I managed to have an awesome time anyway," I answered.

Andrew lifted one eyebrow. "That's funny. I've seen Radio Waves a few times, and I think they're pretty good."

"To each his own." I shrugged and opened a textbook. "By the way, Rachel wasn't at the dance."

As I'd predicted, that remark took Andrew's mind off James Sutton and his stupid band. He looked over at the library desk, and, as if on cue, Rachel Hall walked into the library and took her spot in front of the computer. I saw her glance quickly in our direction, then turn away.

Andrew pushed back his chair. "I just remembered that I forgot to return one of my library books. Be right back."

I leaned back to watch Andrew go to work. I wished he would just ask Rachel out and put himself out of his misery. Andrew handed her a book, then stood wringing his hands for a minute. After exchanging a few sentences with Rachel, he slouched back to our table.

"How did it go?" I asked, thumping him on the back.

"Terrible. I feel like a total idiot around her." He put his head in his hands, but I saw him peer out between his fingers to stare at Rachel.

I decided to let Andrew pout, and turned to my history book. The report was due in a week, and I had a lot to learn about the pharaohs.

"I haven't even been here a semester, and I'm already friends with all the right people," Rebecca said to me Wednesday afternoon. We were sitting in my car, and we'd been kissing for about fifteen minutes.

My stomach tightened in the uncomfortable way it always did when Rebecca mentioned her current level of popularity. At first I'd thought that she just wanted to get to know people. But now she seemed obsessed. I'd even seen her be rude to people who weren't in the "in" crowd.

"That's great," I said flatly. "Now your life is complete."

Rebecca nodded. "And it's all thanks to you." She flipped her long hair over one shoulder and gazed at me flirtatiously. "Thank goodness I found you."

"What do you mean by that?" I kept my tone light, but inside I felt hollow.

"Well, since everybody likes you, they automatically like me. You're my angel."

Over the last few weeks, I'd been convincing myself Rebecca really loved me—and that I loved her. But the doubts I'd been pushing away started flooding into my mind. . . .

Rebecca hadn't shown any interest in getting to

know my friends—unless they happened to be cheerleaders or athletes. And whenever she told me how much she liked me, the word *popularity* seemed to follow in the next sentence. Basically, Rebecca was treating me more like a trophy than a boyfriend.

In a flash, I was hit with the knowledge that I'd forced myself to fall in love with Rebecca because I'd wanted to win my bet with Delia. And as much of a social climber as Rebecca might have been, my motives weren't any purer than hers.

Rebecca's perky voice broke into my reverie. "I think we're the best-looking couple at Jefferson. Don't you?"

I nodded mutely, feeling as if my whole world were crumbling around me.

Thursday night Delia and I were hanging out in the Byrnes' den, watching *An Affair to Remember*. The movie was another of our favorites, and I felt relaxed for the first time since Rebecca had referred to me as her "angel."

Delia was staring silently at the television set, mechanically shoving popcorn into her mouth. Although I wasn't thrilled at the prospect of having Delia rub my nose in the fact that I might lose the bet, I still wanted to talk to her about Rebecca. After all, she was my best friend, and she knew a lot more about women than I did.

"Deels, I think Rebecca is sort of a social climber," I said, taking a handful of popcorn.

"No kidding," Delia responded, sighing.

"Well, I'm thinking that maybe I'm not as much in love with her as I thought."

"Hmm," Delia said absently.

"Deels, are you listening to me?" I poked her.

"Do you think James could still be in love with Tanya?" she asked, instead of answering my question.

"Delia, I just told you that I may not be in love with Rebecca anymore."

She put down the popcorn and looked at me. "The thing is, Ms. Heinsohn called on James to read aloud the poem he'd written." Delia evidently had no interest in what I was trying to say.

"So?"

She frowned. "It was a love poem."

"Please, spare me the details." I wasn't in the mood to hear about James Suckface's flowery poetry.

"The poem wasn't about me, Cain."

"What?" I had to admit that my curiosity was piqued.

"Well, the words were all about loss and 'cruel distance,' as he put it." Delia bit her lip, shaking her head.

"And?" I had a feeling she was leading up to something.

"I think he may have written the poem for Tanya—which would mean that he's not really in love with me." I could have sworn I saw a tear glistening in her eye.

"The guy's a sleazebag. You'd be better off if he *is* still in love with Tanya."

A thought suddenly occurred to me. If Delia broke up with James, and I broke up with Rebecca, then we'd still be even in terms of the bet. Who knew? Maybe I'd fall in love again before the Winter Ball. Anything was possible.

"James is not a sleazebag!" Delia shouted. "If you say that one more time, I'm going to rip your head off. Just shut up!"

I was getting totally fed up with Delia. She'd just said herself that James was still into his ex-girlfriend. If that didn't qualify him as a sleazebag, what did?

"Fine. What *would* you like me to say?"

Delia threw herself back against the couch. "Tanya is coming home for Thanksgiving. Do you think I should be worried?"

"If you don't want me to tell you that James is a sleazebag, then I don't have a comment," I said testily.

Delia buried her face in a sofa pillow. "Cain, would you mind taking off? I really want to be alone." She clicked off the television set and closed her eyes.

Without saying good-bye, I stomped out of the house. I'd wanted to have a serious conversation with Delia, and all she cared about was herself and that wimp she called a boyfriend.

As I sped toward home I started thinking of Rebecca in a whole new light. She might have a few problems, but what person didn't? At least she was always happy to see me—and she never kicked me out of her house.

I made a U-turn. In fact, Rebecca would probably be happy to see me right that second.

Chapter Eleven

Delia

Sunday, November 19
*In the middle of
a boring afternoon . . .*

The weather is bitter cold now. My mood isn't much better. Since James read his infamous poem aloud in creative writing, Ellen and I have analyzed its possible significance over and over again. Now, with the threat of Tanya Reed hanging over my head, I'm acting more and more possessive of James. I don't like myself this way.

James hasn't mentioned her name recently, and of course I didn't ask him about the poem. That would have been the ultimate in humiliation. I have to confess, it's situations like the one I'm in now that kept me from falling in love in the first place. But everything will be okay. I hope.

*   *   *

The Wednesday before Thanksgiving, Jefferson High had let out at noon, and we didn't have to be back in class until Monday. After school I found James next to his locker, where he was hanging out with one of his band members. When I got near, they both stopped talking and turned to look at me. "Are we still on for tomorrow night?" I asked, putting my arm around his waist.

"I wouldn't miss it," he answered, dropping a kiss on my head. Wearing black jeans and a bright plaid shirt, he looked incredible.

"See you at eight o'clock." I walked down the hall, feeling better than I had since I'd heard that idiotic poem.

If James wanted to spend time with Tanya, he wouldn't have agreed to come over to my house on Thanksgiving night. As Ellen had insisted, I was just being paranoid.

It was Thursday evening, and my mom and I were setting the table for our traditional turkey dinner. "So Cain's not coming over tonight?" my mom asked, handing me a stack of our good dishes.

I shook my head. Cain usually came by our house on all major holidays, but this year we'd conveniently forgotten that tradition. Ever since our argument during *An Affair to Remember* the week before, our friendship hadn't been the same.

"He and James aren't really friends," I said. I put the plates around the table, leaving plenty of room for the silver candlesticks that my mom always put out on special occasions.

"That's too bad," my mother said. "Grandma was looking forward to seeing Cain. She says he always makes her laugh and forget the pain of her arthritis."

I shrugged. "Well, she should be happy to meet James. I mean, *he's* the one who's my boyfriend."

"Don't get your feathers ruffled, pumpkin. I'm sure Grandma and Grandpa are ecstatic about meeting James. I was just observing that they'd also like to see Cain."

"Maybe at Christmas, Mom."

When the phone rang, I got a sinking feeling in the pit of my stomach—it must have been my woman's intuition. I answered the phone in the kitchen on the second ring, my hands shaking slightly.

"Hello?"

"Hey, Delia," James said. His voice was as sexy as usual.

"Hi, James." I forced myself to take a deep breath. Maybe he was calling to see if he could bring us anything.

"Listen, I'm not going to be able to make it tonight."

I tried to keep the disappointment out of my voice. "That's too bad. Are your parents giving you a hard time or something?"

I looked over at my mom, who was pretending not to listen to my conversation.

"Ah, yeah. You know how it is. My grandparents are here and everything."

114

"Yeah. Mine are visiting, too." I stretched the telephone cord as far as I could, trying to get out of my mother's earshot.

"I'll call you this weekend?"

"Sure." As I hung up the phone I braced myself for my mom's comments. I figured that at the very least she'd point out that Cain had never canceled on me at the last minute.

But instead of saying anything to me, my mom pushed open the kitchen's swinging door. "Dinner's ready," she yelled. "Turn off the game."

Sitting down at my place, I took stock of the huge pile of sliced turkey that was resting on the platter beside my father's plate. That poor turkey wasn't in any better shape than I was. Suddenly I lost my appetite.

When the doorbell rang, I jumped up from the table and raced out to the front hall. I fully expected to see James, possibly with a bouquet of flowers in his hand. Instead I found Cain. He was holding a pumpkin pie, and there was a light dusting of snow on his jacket.

"Special delivery for the Byrne family," he said, stepping inside.

Impulsively I reached out and gave him a hug. I'd forgotten that I could always count on Cain to improve my mood—even when I was determined to be depressed.

"Shouldn't you be taking your mom's home-made pie to Rebecca's?" I asked.

He unzipped his parka and pulled it off. "They

115

went to New York to see friends. Besides, you don't think I'd let a tradition slide, do you?" He pulled at my ponytail and headed for the dining room.

"Cain Parson!" I heard my grandmother exclaim. "Is it snowing outside?"

Cain walked over to my grandma and gave her a kiss on the cheek. "It just started this very minute, Mrs. Byrne. Mother Nature must have heard you all were coming to town."

As I've said before, Cain has a natural ability to put people at ease. And no matter how bad his jokes were, my grandmother always laughed as if he were Johnny Carson.

"You kids," she said. "I'm glad to see you in here. Delia's been moping around as if she'd just seen her last sunrise."

Cain looked over my family's heads and raised his eyebrows. I shrugged.

"Don't just stand there with that dessert in your hand," my dad interrupted. "Go get yourself a plate."

As Cain headed into the kitchen I moved over to the table. All of a sudden, pumpkin pie sounded like the perfect remedy for my particular case of the blues.

"Let's go for a walk in the snow," Cain said to me an hour later.

We were all sitting around the fireplace in our den, having finished off the pie Cain had brought as well as part of one that my mom had made. My grandparents were dozing in their armchairs, and my dad looked as if he was about to follow suit.

Outside, snow was falling heavily, and our lawn was already coated with a layer of gleaming white.

"You may as well enjoy it now," my mom agreed. "By tomorrow it could all be slush."

"I could definitely use some exercise after all that pie," I said, throwing off the quilt in which I'd bundled myself.

Cain followed me out to the front hall, and I retrieved both of our parkas. While I zipped mine up, he rummaged through our hall closet, where we keep a basket of assorted hats, scarves, mittens, and gloves. He pulled out an old purple and green striped hat (complete with a fuzzy ball on top) and stuck it on my head.

"Hey, I'm not wearing this," I said. "I'll stop traffic."

Cain wiggled his eyebrows. "If you wear *that,* I'll wear *this,*" he said. He brought his hand out from behind his back and revealed a bright orange hat that my father had bought for his one and only hunting trip. The hat had ear flaps, and it said "Deer me, don't shoot!" across the bill.

I giggled, winding an old scarf around my neck. "Now that's an offer I can't refuse! Let's go scare the neighbors."

Cain pulled the front door shut behind us, and we tramped across the lawn, kicking up snow as we went. At the street we turned left. There's an almost deserted road a couple of blocks from my house, and I knew we were heading toward it.

For several minutes neither of us spoke. The snow was coming down heavily, but since there wasn't much wind I felt warm and cozy in my down jacket. Every few moments I stuck out my tongue to taste a fresh snowflake. Cain was zigzagging back and forth across the street, trying to generate as many footprints as possible.

"Maybe we should have called Andrew," I said to break the silence.

Cain shrugged. "He probably wouldn't have wanted to come over. I think he's secretly spending his nights studying pictures of Rachel Hall in old yearbooks."

"Why doesn't he just ask her out already?" I asked, kicking a rock out of my way.

"He says it's because he doesn't want to tie himself down, but my guess is that he's scared of rejection. I don't think he's ever really cared before whether or not a girl said yes to a date."

I nodded. "We can all relate to that feeling," I commented.

"Would you rather be with James?" Cain asked suddenly, walking in a wide circle around me.

I didn't answer right away. In the last hour and a half I'd completely forgotten my earlier disappointment over James's having broken our date. Being with Cain seemed like the perfect way to enjoy the snow and the festive feeling in the air.

"No, I'm glad to be with you," I said finally. "Why? Are you pining away for Rebecca?"

Cain scooped up a handful of snow and packed it into a ball. "Nah. Rebecca's not much fun to throw snowballs at!"

As Cain threw the snowball at me I heard his laugh ring out in the dark night. The snow hit me directly in the face, and I squealed loudly. Right away I knelt down and used both my arms to scoop up as much snow as I could. Running over to where Cain was laughing, I dumped my armful down his back.

He screamed, desperately trying to shake out his jacket. "That was a declaration of war!" he cried.

We'd reached the quiet road near my house, and there was undisturbed snow everywhere. For the next fifteen minutes we acted like lunatics, throwing snowballs and tackling each other to the ground. During the whole battle, I was laughing so hard that my sides ached.

Finally we collapsed next to each other on the ground. I was so exhausted that all I could do was stare up at the sky and catch my breath. When I became aware that my butt was wet and painfully cold, I turned to Cain and said, "That felt good, but I think it's time to seek shelter in the form of hot chocolate."

"First let's make snow angels," Cain suggested. "I haven't done that in years." He lay back beside me and started flapping his arms and legs.

"There's not enough snow on the ground to made good angels," I countered. "We'd need at least six inches."

Cain put a handful of snow in his mouth and made a slurping noise. "So what? It's the thought that counts."

I couldn't argue with his logic, so I made the best snow angel I could, then stood up to survey the results. "Not bad, considering."

"Not bad at all," Cain agreed. "Now, did I hear someone say *hot chocolate*—the key word being *hot?*"

Minutes later we stood in my kitchen, breathless. We were both pulling off our boots, socks, and sweaters, trying to find something on us that was still dry. Cain's damp hair stood up straight in places, and his lips had a bluish tinge.

Everyone else had gone to sleep, so I tiptoed to the laundry room and found Cain a pair of my dad's sweatpants and a sweatshirt. Then I went to my room and changed into flannel pajamas. By the time we sat down with our hot chocolate next to the glowing embers of the fire, we were both warm and dry.

Out of nowhere, Cain let out a deep sigh.

"What's that for?" I asked.

"I don't know. I was just thinking that tonight really is the perfect night for romance."

I stared into the fire, wondering if James was snuggled up with Tanya somewhere, drinking hot chocolate and telling her how much he had missed her. I felt a lump rise in my throat, and I swallowed hard. "Yeah," I whispered. "I know what you mean."

When Cain turned to me, his eyes looked almost black. He inched closer to me on the couch, then wound a few strands of my hair around his index finger. My heart started beating quickly, and I felt the same confused emotions that I'd experienced at the homecoming dance.

"You know that song?" he asked quietly.

I shook my head, unable to tear my eyes away from his. "What song?"

"'If you can't be with the one you love . . .'"

"'Love the one you're with,'" I finished. My gaze dropped to his red lips, and I felt mesmerized by his closeness.

Cain put one hand at the back of my head and gently pulled me closer. I closed my eyes, willing his lips to touch mine.

As soon as I felt his kiss, a liquid fire spread through me. Without thinking, I clutched at the fabric of his sweatshirt, not wanting to let him go. The fireworks that I'd been hoping for with James finally went off in my head. Every inch of my skin was alive and burning as if I'd been put in the middle of a nuclear fission experiment. The outside world evaporated, and Cain was the only thing—living or dead—that still existed on the planet.

A moment later he pulled away.

As soon as the kiss was over, I felt a wave of humiliation sweep over me. Had I done that? Had I just kissed Cain, my best friend in the world? A million questions raced around in my head, and I was speechless.

"Wow, I don't know if that was such a hot idea," he said, raking his fingers through his hair.

My sense of bewilderment was quickly replaced with anger. "Why did you do that?" I hissed.

"What do you mean, *me?*" he asked. "You were here, too."

I balled my hands into fists. "It was your idea. Don't deny it." I was trying to keep my voice down, but I felt like screaming.

Cain glared at me. "Well, it was obviously a very *bad* idea," he said, punching the sofa with his fist.

"You just can't stand the fact that there's one girl in this town who doesn't want to go out with you," I said.

"Don't flatter yourself, Delia. It'll never happen again."

"Good!" I crossed my arms in front of my chest.

"Good!" he said back to me, standing up. "Tell your dad thanks for the clothes. I'll get them back to him as soon as possible."

"Don't do us any favors," I said, stalking to the front hall.

"Don't worry. I won't." He grabbed his still-wet jacket and yanked it on.

"Fine by me." I opened the door and stared at him. My hands were trembling, and I felt dangerously close to tears.

"Give your grandparents my regards," Cain said.

Then he stepped out into the snowy night, and I slammed the door behind him. At that point I really didn't care if I woke up the whole house. The day had been one of the worst in my life, and all I wanted to do was curl up and cry myself to sleep.

As I listened to Cain start his car and back out of the driveway, the tears I'd been holding in started rolling down my cheeks. I stumbled to my room, choking on sobs that felt as if they'd never quit.

Once again I'd gone and made a big, fat mess of my life. "Why me?" I whispered into the darkness. "Why me?"

Chapter Twelve

Cain

WHEN I OPENED my eyes Friday morning, I knew there was something wrong. But it took me a few moments to piece together the disastrous events of the previous night. Then I remembered kissing Delia.

I groaned, lightly knocking my head against the wall above my bed. In one fell swoop, I'd broken the cardinal rule of a platonic friendship. Now Delia hated me, and there was nothing I could do about it.

I replayed the scene over and over in my mind. What had made me kiss her? Was it the snow? The fireplace? I shook my head. The reasons were too painful to contemplate—not to mention irrelevant. I'd screwed up a good thing, and no amount of rationalization was going to change that.

There was also the matter of Rebecca. Technically speaking, I'd cheated on her. Even if kissing Delia had taken place during a moment of temporary insanity, there was no denying that the kiss had taken place— not that Rebecca would ever find out.

Another question plagued me. If Rebecca did find out about the kiss, would she care? Sure, her pride would be hurt. But would she be truly upset—or just angry? She'd told me she'd call from me from New York, but so far I hadn't heard from her. Was she visiting an old boyfriend?

The idea that she might possibly be kissing some other guy was oddly comforting. While I wasn't crazy about the image of my girlfriend locked in the arms of a slick New Yorker, the mental picture did allay my guilt. Rebecca and I were young—it was understandable that we would both make mistakes. Right? Right.

Having resolved that issue, my thoughts shifted from the Rebecca problem back to the Delia problem. But before I could compose a decent apology, my mom knocked on the door.

"Cain? Are you awake?" she called, opening the door a crack.

"Unfortunately, yes." I rolled back onto my stomach, hoping she would take the hint and go away.

"Delia's downstairs, honey."

"She is?" I sat up quickly and pushed my comforter to the foot of the bed. "Give me two minutes, then send her up."

I hopped around my room, trying to pull on my jeans and comb my hair at the same time. The door opened as I was buttoning up my shirt, and Delia stuck her head in the room.

124

"Can I convince you to give your former best friend a moment of your time?" she asked.

Right away the sick feeling I'd had since I woke up disappeared. Delia's voice sounded friendly; everything was going to be okay. "Only if you'll delete the 'former' from that question," I answered, opening the door all the way.

"I've brought a peace offering," Delia said, stepping into my room. She handed me a box of doughnuts and flopped into the old recliner I kept in my room.

"You know, Deels, I woke up this morning with one thing on my mind: French crullers. And now here you are."

"I know you too well, Parson." Delia swung her legs over the side of the chair and rested her head on her hands. "I didn't get much sleep last night."

"Me neither. I felt like I'd just come face-to-face with the apocalypse." I grabbed a doughnut and held the box out to Delia.

She took a French cruller, then ate half of it in one bite. "We can't let this ruin our friendship. We both overreacted."

"I couldn't agree more," I said.

In the light of day, the whole incident didn't seem like such a big deal. We'd kissed. One kiss hardly equaled the end of the world. After all, we were red-blooded American teenagers. Teenagers kissed all the time. It wasn't as if we'd committed murder or something.

Delia chewed thoughtfully for a moment. "I

125

mean, if we'd actually *enjoyed* kissing each other, then we might have a problem."

I nodded, wondering where she was going with her little speech. I could always tell when a theory was brewing in Delia's mind.

"But when you think about the whole scenario rationally, you realize that our kissing was almost a *good* thing." She paused for a moment, waiting for my reaction. When I didn't say anything, she continued. "Here we are, two friends of the opposite sex. It's *natural* that we would have a certain amount of, uh, curiosity about each other."

"Curiosity," I repeated, just to let her know I was listening.

"Yeah. And now that we have our kiss out of the way, we can let the whole matter fade into the forgotten past. We know we never want to kiss each other again, and we won't. End of story."

I was a little upset that she could dismiss my kiss so easily. For me the experience had been like shooting through space, clinging to the back of a runaway rocket ship. When I'd finally pulled away, it had taken at least ten seconds for me to realize that, yes, gravity still existed. I couldn't deny that she'd excited me—to a dangerous level.

But I wasn't about to argue with her. At that point I probably would have agreed if she'd said that the earth was actually flat. I just wanted us to make up and move on. "End of story," I confirmed.

Delia stuck out her hand, and I shook it firmly. "Well, I'm glad we got *that* resolved," she said, as if she were referring to an argument over who had to wash the dishes.

I gave her a smile. "Me too, Deels. I'm sure we'll both sleep much better tonight."

"Oh, yes. Absolutely."

"Definitely." I leaned back against my pillows, feeling as if I'd been reborn. My world wasn't going to crumble after all, and I couldn't have been more grateful.

I had butterflies in my stomach as I drove to Rebecca's Sunday evening. She'd called me as soon as she'd gotten back from New York that afternoon, and now I was just minutes from seeing her beautiful face. I'd been thrilled to hear her voice, especially because I felt as if we were going to have a brand-new start. Since the whole kissing episode with Delia, I'd realized that I must have been missing Rebecca more than I'd thought. Obviously I'd projected those feelings onto Delia, who had in turn projected her feelings for James onto me—all in all, a recipe for exactly what had ended up happening.

By Sunday the temperature was still below freezing. So when Rebecca had asked if I wanted to go ice skating at Hamilton Park, I thought the idea was inspired. I imagined the two of us holding hands, circling the pond. Aside from any little kids in our path, we'd be in our own world. Afterward, we'd go back to her house, drink hot chocolate (actually, maybe hot cider would be a better idea), and kiss far into the night. I couldn't wait.

When I arrived at the Fosters', Rebecca opened the door immediately. Before I could even give her a hello kiss, she twirled around in the front hallway.

"Ta-da! How do you like my new skating outfit?" she asked.

"Wow!" I couldn't think of anything else to say.

Rebecca was wearing a short pink skating dress. The material must have been one hundred percent Lycra, because the dress clung to her as if it were a second skin. Her long legs were covered with flesh-colored tights, and she was already holding her pristine white skates in one hand. To be honest, everyone I knew ice-skated in jeans and sweaters— it had never occurred to me that Rebecca would be outfitted for a leading role in the Ice Capades. But I wasn't about to complain. She looked like an Olympic athlete turned supermodel.

"Let's get going. Everybody will be there soon." She grabbed her coat and skipped out the door.

I didn't know what she meant by "everybody," but I was still speechless from the aftereffects of her dress. If I opened my mouth, I was sure that my voice would come out as a squeak.

In the sanctuary of my car, I pulled Rebecca close. Kissing her would be the final step toward erasing that horrible night with Delia. Once my lips touched Rebecca's, Thanksgiving night would be nothing more than a bad dream. At least, that's what I hoped.

Rebecca felt warm and vital in my arms, and the smooth fabric of her dress was like silk beneath my fingers. I kissed her lips, then her cheek, then her forehead. I wasn't flying through space at the speed of light, but I *was* fully aware of all my hormones.

I kissed Rebecca harder, struggling to undo my kiss with Delia. After a few breathless minutes, I decided that the explosion I'd felt with Delia had been due to the fact that I'd been missing my girl-friend—and worried that she was with someone else in New York. I'd just been releasing pent-up emotions. There were all sorts of psychological explanations. The mind was a powerful thing . . . wasn't that what people were always saying?

Rebecca ruffled my hair, giggling. "I've only been gone four days," she said. "You seem like a guy who's just walked through the desert with no canteen."

I kissed her again. "That's how I feel."

"Well, I'm glad you appreciate me. Not every girl would go see her ex-boyfriends in New York and resist all of their pleas to get back together."

I glanced quickly at Rebecca, marveling at the way women always knew exactly what to say in order to make a guy feel like a complete jerk. I was glad that the light outside was fading fast, because I was positive that a guilty flush was spreading across my cheeks. "We'd better take off," I said.

The parking lot at Hamilton Park was half full, and I recognized a few of the cars that were already there. Suddenly I had a sinking feeling who Rebecca had meant by "everybody."

"The whole gang is here!" she cried happily as we made our way to the crowded pond.

"You didn't tell me that half of Jefferson High

was going skating tonight," I said, a little more sharply than I'd intended.

"Isn't it great? I'm so excited to see everybody!" She ran ahead of me, disappearing behind the hut where people could rent ice skates.

A few seconds later I heard Rebecca squeal. When she came into view, she was hugging Carrie Starks as if the girl were her long-lost sister. I gagged mentally. Despite Rebecca's love for cheerleaders such as Carrie Starks and Amanda Wright, I thought both girls were superficial and stupid at best, and backbiting and manipulative at worst. They were the kind of girls who made you give them a kiss on the cheek by way of greeting. But they were always too impatient to actually wait for your lips to make contact, so you ended up kissing the air.

Sure enough, Carrie ran up to me. "Aren't you going to give me a kiss, Cain?" she asked, stepping close. Lips puckered, I bent down. As expected, I gave the spot where her cheek had been a loud, but futile, smack.

Rebecca tugged me toward the pond, where I pulled my hockey skates out of the bag I was carrying. As I saw Patrick Mayor, Bart Langley, and Josh Nielson, my dreams of a romantic evening with Rebecca evaporated. My opinion of Patrick hadn't improved since the night of his party, when I'd seen Delia locked in an almost indecent embrace with James. And I absolutely *hated* Josh Nielson.

Josh had had a thing for Delia during our sophomore year of high school. She went out with him once, detested him, and never wanted to speak to him again. A total Neanderthal, Josh had taken to being incredibly cruel to her at school. When Delia didn't respond to his baiting, Josh wrote graffiti about her on the walls of the guys' locker room. One day I caught him in the act, which led to the only fistfight I've ever had. After the coach pulled us apart, I swore to myself that I'd never punch anyone again. The next year, Josh switched schools when his parents moved to another district, and I'd been able to avoid him ever since. (Delia, by the way, never found out about the fight.)

I laced up my skates quickly, telling myself that after a year and a half, Josh had probably evolved into a human being. As long I was nice to him, we wouldn't have an ugly scene.

Rebecca was already on the ice, skating in big figure eights around the pond. I took a few deep breaths and joined her, determined to keep my cool.

I took Rebecca's hand, and we circled the pond. Ignoring the presence of Josh Nielson, I actually started to enjoy myself.

"This is so romantic," Rebecca said, looking up at the stars and the bright, full moon.

"That's because you're here," I answered, taking both of Rebecca's hands and spinning her around in a circle.

I did a quick hockey stop when I saw Josh Nielson out of the corner of my eye. He was headed straight for us, and he was sneering. I gritted my teeth and forced my expression to be relaxed and friendly.

"Hey, Josh," I said. "Do you know Rebecca Foster?"

His eyes traveled the length of her body, and he gave her an oily smile. "Only through the grapevine till now. Nice to meet you, Rebecca."

She gave him a flirtatious smile. "How come I haven't met you before?"

"I go to Rosedale High. But I like to keep in touch with my old friends." Josh looked at me, and I could tell from the light in his eyes that he was dying to tell me something.

Positive that I wasn't interested in anything he had to say, I took Rebecca's hand again. "Shall we pick up where we left off?" I asked her, nodding good-bye to Josh.

At that moment he put a hand on my shoulder, stopping me. "Speaking of old friends, Mayor told me that our mutual sweetheart, Delia Byrne, is going out with James Sutton."

I saw Rebecca narrow her eyes, and I didn't blame her. Josh had made it sound as if Delia and I were an item. But I didn't want to push the point; I decided to explain the situation to Rebecca later. "Yep. They're totally in love," I said, satisfied to see his sneer turn into a frown.

"Well, you might pass a message from me to her," Josh said.

"What's that?" I could feel the muscles in my back tense up, but I refused to let him know he was getting to me.

"I saw James and Tanya Reed looking very friendly at Jon's Pizzeria the other night. In fact, they were making out in a corner." He grinned at me, then laughed.

"You're lying."

"I couldn't care less if you believe me, Parson. But you really should tell your friend that Sutton was just using her until he could get his hands on Tanya again."

I was trembling with anger, and I couldn't stop myself from taking a step closer to Nielson. Whether or not he was telling the truth, I wanted to wipe the smile off his face.

"You're just jealous because Delia wouldn't go out with your pathetic self," I said angrily.

"Delia's a loser," Josh countered. "Ask anyone."

Then Rebecca decided to contribute her thoughts on the subject. "He does have a point, Cain. Everyone knows that Delia's sort of . . . strange."

"Thanks for your opinion, Rebecca. But this conversation is between Josh and me."

"Want to fight, Parson?" Josh asked, sticking his face close to mine.

"You're not worth it," I answered. I noticed that Patrick and Bart had skated up to us, and they were exchanging curious glances.

While I was looking away, Josh seized his opportunity. Out of nowhere, his fist hit me squarely on the chin. I fell backward, landing on my butt with a groan.

"Delia's the coolest woman I know," I shouted. "She puts any girlfriend you could get to shame."

As I tried to regain my footing, Josh lunged. But before he could punch me again, Patrick and Bart grabbed him. They pulled him several feet away, not letting go of his arms.

"I think this skating party is over," Bart said. He and Patrick hauled Josh off the ice.

I stood up on the ice, still furious. As I averted my eyes from Josh I saw that Rebecca was glowering at me, her hands on her hips.

"If you like Delia so much, maybe you should go out with her!" Rebecca yelled. "You two deserve each other."

I just stared at Rebecca, too shocked to speak.

When I didn't say anything, she gave me a cold smile. "We're through."

I watched her skate away, feeling like a balloon that had just been popped. When she got to the edge of the pond, she untied her skates and jogged toward the parking lot. "Josh, wait up," I heard her yell. Then I couldn't see her anymore.

I sank back down on the ice, too exhausted to move. I was hurt that Rebecca had broken up with me, but I guess deep down I'd known our relationship was doomed. She'd always had more in common with Carrie and Amanda than I'd wanted to admit; now I could see how superficial she really was.

Cold wind whistled in my ears, but otherwise the night was silent. I'd reached the end of Thanksgiving vacation—and the end of my relationship with Rebecca Foster.

I gazed around the now-empty pond, shaking my head. "I guess this means I lost the bet," I said aloud.

Chapter Thirteen

Delia

WHEN ELLEN AND I walked into creative writing Monday morning, my palms were sweaty and I had a queasy feeling in my stomach. I hadn't talked to James since Thanksgiving night, and I'd spent most of Sunday evening explaining to myself all the good reasons he could have for not calling me. For one thing, his grandparents were in town. I also knew that Radio Waves had a gig at a local community college soon; they were probably practicing every day. I even took Thursday night's snowfall into account—maybe he'd used half his Friday shoveling the driveway.

Still, my hands trembled at the thought of seeing him. The pessimistic Delia had burst through, as strong as ever. I almost expected him to be wearing a sign that said, "I spent the weekend making out with Tanya Reed."

"I'm sure he was just busy," Ellen said soothingly. "Tanya Reed has nothing on you. She's all style, no substance."

"Oh, I feel much better now," I said wryly. "Everyone knows that seventeen-year-old guys prefer substance to style. What planet are you on, anyway?"

Ellen shrugged. "Hey, at least I'm looking at the bright side."

"There is no bright side," I responded glumly.

When Ellen and I sat down, there was no sign of James. Ms. Heinsohn asked us to pass in our short-story assignments, and I opened my notebook, keeping one eye glued to the door.

"What's your story about?" Ellen asked, peering over at my notebook.

"Nothing. It's really stupid," I said quickly.

My story was about a guy and girl who were best friends. One night they kissed by a romantic fire, and it almost ruined their friendship. At the end of the story, they made up. The plot wasn't exactly original, but everyone said that writing was supposed to be cathartic. I'd figured that putting what had happened with Cain down on paper would be good therapy, and strangely enough, it had been.

I turned to Ellen. "How about you?"

"Mine's stupid, too," she answered.

I sneaked a glance at the story Ellen was holding. Using all capital letters, she'd written the title on the top of the first page: "HELP! I HAVE A CRUSH ON MY BEST FRIEND'S BEST FRIEND!" From the title I had a pretty good idea of what her story was about. If Ms. Heinsohn had half a brain, she'd probably notice the striking similarities between the male protagonists of our stories. I sighed. Monday was not shaping up well at all.

Five minutes after the bell rang, James walked in. He smiled an apology to Ms. Heinsohn and slid into a chair next to the door. I tried to catch his eye, but he was concentrating on the handout the teacher had put on his desk.

For the next fifteen minutes I forced myself to keep my head turned from where James was sitting. If he wasn't going to acknowledge me, I wasn't about to make doe eyes at him from across the room. *It's over,* I repeated to myself again and again. *He's still in love with Tanya.*

When Ellen tapped my shoulder, I practically jumped out of my chair. She handed me a folded-up note and jerked her head in James's direction.

My pulse racing, I opened the note: "Delia. Meet me right after school? Love, James."

I glanced up and saw that he'd been watching me. I nodded and smiled, then turned back to Ms. Heinsohn. My heart soared. Maybe he really *did* have a good reason for not calling me. For now, I had to hope for the best.

"I can't talk long," I said to James, pulling shut the passenger-side door of his Jeep. "I have to be at Nina Johnson's in half an hour."

In a black turtleneck sweater and faded blue jeans, James looked as handsome as usual. His eyes were bright, almost glowing. *He's happy to see me!* I said to myself. A pleasurable tingle traveled up my spine.

137

Finally everything was going to get back to normal.

"I'm sorry I didn't call you this weekend," he said quietly.

I shrugged, trying to seem as if I hadn't even noticed that the phone had been silently mocking me for three whole days. "Oh, that's okay. I was really busy with my grandparents."

James nodded. "Yeah, I was pretty busy too. . . ."

I decided to look fear in the face and ask him about his old girlfriend. If the past was the past, then I had no reason to be jealous. "So, did you get a chance to see Tanya this weekend?" I asked casually. "I heard she was in town."

James bit his lip and stared at his steering wheel as if it were a Picasso painting instead of a few pounds of metal and plastic. "Uh, yeah. That's actually why I was so busy."

"Oh." There was nothing more to say. I could have gotten out of the car and never heard another word from James. The combination of guilt and excitement in his voice told me everything I needed to know. All of a sudden I was facing the very real possibility of throwing up.

Like a fool, I didn't get out of the car. I just sat in stunned silence, waiting for him to say something.

"She didn't meet anyone at school. And she really missed me. . . . I guess I missed her, too."

"Oh," I said again. Tears were threatening to spill out of my eyes, and I blinked rapidly. I wasn't about to let James Sutton see how humiliated and hurt I was.

"We're going to try out a long-distance relationship," he continued. "It's not that I don't love you—I think you're great. But Tanya and I—we're fated to be together."

I swallowed hard and sat up as straight as I could in the seat of the Jeep. "I think that's wonderful, James," I said. Amazingly, my voice sounded smooth and natural.

"It is?" He sounded surprised.

"Yes. Because there's something I wanted to tell you, too." I stuck my hands in the pockets of my coat so he couldn't see that they were shaking.

"There is?" Again he sounded surprised. His beautiful eyebrows were raised, and he was now staring me straight in the eye.

"Yeah. This weekend Cain and I realized that we're in love." Even as I was saying the words I didn't believe that they were coming from my lips. *Sorry, Cain,* I thought silently.

"Oh." I felt a glimmer of satisfaction that James seemed slightly off balance.

"Isn't this the funniest coincidence?" I said lightly. "We're both so lucky that we didn't have to hurt the other person."

"Yeah," James agreed, looking confused.

"I guess I'll see you around." I leaned over and gave him a kiss on the cheek. Then I opened the door and got out of the car.

"Bye, Delia."

"Bye, James," I said, slamming the door behind me.

It wasn't until he pulled out of the parking lot that my knees buckled and I fell to the ground, sobbing.

*　　　*　　　*

Usually I enjoyed baby-sitting Nina. But that afternoon felt more like a prison sentence than a job. She was firing questions at me at a rate of one per second, most having to do with boy-girl relationships.

"Marcy Stein is having a party this Friday," she said. We were sitting in the Johnsons' den, and I was helping her with a school art project.

"That's nice," I responded vacantly. I was in no mood to talk about parties.

"And she's having boys," Nina continued. She seemed to be holding her breath, waiting for my response.

"How thrilling." I realized right away that I wasn't being fair to Nina, and the hurt look on her face sent a fresh wave of pain over me. "I'm sorry," I said, hugging her. "I'm sure you'll have a great time."

Nina was young, but she wasn't stupid. She knew I wasn't telling her something. "What's wrong, Delia? You look sad."

I shrugged, fighting back tears. "James and I broke up today. I guess I've got the blues."

"I didn't like James anyway," she said, as if her declaration settled the matter.

"You never even met him," I pointed out.

"I know. But Cain told me about him." She cut out a construction-paper heart and wrote her initials inside.

"And what did Cain say?"

"He said James was a wimp and that you deserved someone better."

I almost laughed. Since when did Cain discuss my love life with a ten-year-old? "Cain shouldn't have said that. Who I go out with is none of his business. Or yours." I watched as Nina added another set of initials to her heart, deducing that H.R. must have been her latest crush.

"He was right, though. Wasn't he?" She looked up at me, her blue eyes wide and trusting.

"Yeah," I sighed. "I guess he was."

I stood on the Parsons' front stoop, shivering with cold. I'd been in such a rush that I hadn't bothered to grab my coat.

"Delia!" The second Cain saw me, he enveloped me in a huge hug. "I'm sorry," he whispered in my ear.

I wiped my tears on the sleeve of his sweater and looked up into his face. "How did you know?"

"From the expression on your face, I could tell that either someone in your family had died or you and James had broken up. Since your mother sounded fine when I just talked to her on the phone, I made an educated guess."

I covered my face with my hands and threw myself on the Parsons' living room sofa. "I feel terrible."

"I know how you feel." He sat down next to me and patted my back awkwardly.

I sniffled. "How do you know how I feel?"

"Rebecca dumped me when we went skating on Sunday," he said, his voice neutral.

"Why?" This news was shocking enough to make me forget my own misery for a second.

"Who knows?" He slumped back on the sofa, looking uncomfortable.

141

"I never liked her." I sympathized with Cain, but I wouldn't miss having to play nice with Queen Rebecca.

"And I never liked James."

"Speaking of James, I told him something really, really stupid." I decided I might as well confess. Cain was bound to hear that I'd announced we were in love.

"What?" he asked.

"Promise you won't get mad."

"What? Tell me." His voice was impatient, and I didn't want him to get any more irritated before I spilled my guts.

"Well, when James told me he and Tanya were getting back together, I was totally humiliated. . . ."

"And?" Cain pressed.

"And so to save face I told him that you and I were in love." I stared at a vase on the mantelpiece, waiting for his burst of anger. To my surprise, he laughed.

"Who cares?" he said.

"Really?" At least that was one worry off my mind.

"Sure. People are always saying we're in love—you know that. In a week we'll just tell everyone that we decided we were better off friends, and that'll be that."

For the first time since James broke up with me, I smiled. "You're right! What we do is no one's business, anyway."

Cain nodded. "And I can't wait to see the look on Rebecca's face! It'll be a real Kodak moment."

Chapter Fourteen

Cain

Thursday, November 30
11:30 P.M.

I saw Rebecca flirting with Patrick Mayor in the hall today. And you know what? I didn't feel anything—well, maybe pity for Patrick (just kidding). Actually, I was a little hurt. Did I mean anything to her at all? Then again, did she really mean anything to me? Maybe Delia's been right all along. Maybe I don't know anything about real love. But who does?

Friday night Delia and I were drowning our sorrows in a banana split at Swenson's. Andrew was with us, but he wasn't saying much. He was just staring into his ice cream as if the future were written in fudge swirl. The three of us were a pretty gloomy bunch.

"You know what your problem is, Delia Byrne?" I asked.

"Yeah, the fact that you always ask me what my problem is," she responded automatically. We'd had a million conversations that started exactly this way.

"Wrong again. Your problem is that you fall in love too easily."

"Ha! This is coming from the man who challenged, even *dared* me to fall in love. What a hypocrite."

"I'm older and wiser now," I responded. "And I've decided that love is strictly off-limits."

She tapped her spoon thoughtfully against the ornate glass bowl our banana split had been served in. "I think I have a suggestion that will make even your jaded self say yes to love again."

I licked another bite of ice cream off my spoon. "I doubt that, but try me."

"You should ask Ellen out." She sat back, looking pleased with herself.

"Ellen Frazier?" I asked, surprised. I knew Ellen had always carried a small torch for me, but I'd never even considered asking her out. I mean, next to me, she was Delia's best friend. Even the idea of going out with her was just too bizarre.

"Of course Ellen Frazier. She's pretty, intelligent, and ten times cooler than any other girl you've dated."

I shook my head. "I think I'll stay on my own, thank you very much."

At that point Andrew looked up from his bowl of ice cream. "I agree with Delia. What do you have to lose?"

I stared at him. "Aren't you the guy who's been dateless for the entire semester?" I asked.

"That's different," he said.

"Why?" I looked at him expectantly, and I could tell that Delia was curious, too. Lately Andrew had been pretty secretive about what was going on his head.

He licked his spoon clean, then patted his mouth with a napkin. "Because *I* am going to ask out Rachel Hall. Soon. Very soon."

I rolled my eyes. "Yeah, right. Just like you were going to ask her out a dozen other times in the last two months."

Andrew blushed a little. "I *would* have asked her out, but I was going through a process of elimination. Now, after studying forty-two different girls at Jefferson High, I've come to the conclusion that Rachel is the only one worth asking out. No offense, Delia."

Delia shrugged. She was used to Andrew's obnoxious comments about women. "You're such a liar," I said. "You haven't asked her out because you've been totally terrified that she'll diss you."

Andrew put some money on the table. "Think whatever you want, Cain. Just take Delia's advice and go out with Ellen. Staying at home alone on Saturday night is *not* fun." He stood. "I'll catch you guys later."

When Andrew was gone, Delia put down her spoon. "Don't say I didn't try. If you die old, gray, and lonely, just remember that Delia tried to help."

"I'll think about it," I conceded. "But right now all my energy is focused on forgetting that

Rebecca Foster ever existed. It's a full-time job."

"We must have the same employer. Long hours, little reward," Delia said. "Finish this." She pushed the nearly empty dish toward me.

I spooned up the rest of the fudge on the bottom of the dish, savoring its sweet taste. "How about we check out what the late, late show is?" I asked after I'd swallowed the fudge.

"Good plan," Delia agreed. "It's Cary Grant week on channel four."

She got up and gathered her coat and hat from the seat of the booth. As I helped her slip into her parka, I caught a glimpse of us in the old-fashioned mirror that hung on the wall next to the booth.

We were both smiling, and I noticed that we looked like every other pair in Swenson's. If I hadn't known better, I'd have thought we were the ultimate high-school couple, young and in love.

Two and a half hours later, Delia used the remote control to turn off the TV set in the Byrnes' den, sighing. We'd just watched *The Philadelphia Story*, and she had a dreamy expression on her face that I'd seen many times before. Despite her hard-edged exterior, Delia has always been a sucker for romance.

"Do you think any guy could love me as much as Jimmy Stewart loved Katharine Hepburn in that movie?" she asked.

"That's a dumb question," I answered.

"Because you think there's no way a guy could ever love me that much?" she asked, her voice sad.

Delia was stretched out on the sofa, and her calves and feet were resting in my lap. When I glanced over at her face, I saw that the dreamy expression had been replaced with one of gloom.

"No, Deels. Because I'm positive that there are a thousand guys who could and will love you just as much as Jimmy loved Kate."

She smiled. "Really? Do you mean that?"

"Delia, you're the most awesome chick at Jefferson High. In the *world*. Any guy would be crazy not to fall in love with you."

She sat up, then reached out and put her arms around me. I returned the hug, relieved that she was smiling again. "I'm so glad you're my best friend," she said, her voice muffled against my shirt.

"Not half as glad as I am," I responded. I squeezed her shoulders, then hugged her even tighter.

"I love you," Delia said, pressing her face against my chest.

"I love you, too. Always."

Delia and I used the *l* word fairly often. Both of us knew that there was a parenthetical "as a friend" attached to the end of the sentence, so we never bothered saying it. But that night the words seemed even more true than they had in the past. I assumed it was because we had both been through a rough time, and we realized more than ever how much we relied on each other's enduring friendship.

Delia tilted up her head and gave me a friendly kiss on the cheek. I moved my head, responding with a kiss on *her* cheek. Then she gave me a kiss on

147

the other side of my face. And I gave her a kiss on the other side of *her* face. We went on and on like that, until we must have exchanged twenty kisses.

Finally, when I went to kiss her cheek, my lips accidentally-on-purpose landed on her mouth. Rather than turn away, I gave her a quick kiss on the lips. Which she returned. Suddenly I found myself kissing her again and again, wanting more and more.

Delia responded, parting her warm lips beneath mine. My fingers became tangled in her hair, and her hands clutched the material of my shirt, bunching it up around my shoulders. I lost track of time, suspended in the burning, electric sensations that spread through my body. I felt as if we were one person, two halves of a whole.

With a start, Delia pulled away. She bolted upright, then collapsed into the chair next to the fireplace. Without warning, she burst into tears. She covered her face with her hands, weeping quietly.

A feeling of helplessness engulfed me, and I stood up. Patting her clumsily on the back, I tried to murmur soothing words.

After a minute or so, she started talking. "With James . . . kiss . . . never . . . I don't . . ."

I could only decipher about one out of every ten words, but it didn't take a genius to see that she was upset about James. It was clear that kissing me had reminded her that the guy she really loved had left her in the cold.

"Delia, don't worry, everything's going to be okay," I said, not knowing whether or not the statement was true.

"It is?" she asked through her tears, looking up at me.

I nodded firmly. "Listen, we're both upset about our breakups. It's not surprising that we turned to each other. I promise, nothing between us has changed."

"You're right," she said, wiping her tears away with her sleeve. "I'm just upset about James, that's all."

She seemed to have regained her composure. I was glad, although I realized even then that I was taken aback that all she could think about was Suckface. I, for one, had thought that our kisses had been pretty explosive. Still, I played my best-friend role like an Oscar-winning actor.

"We're friends. Just like always," I said firmly.

She smiled brightly, then stuck out her hand for me to shake. "Friends," she repeated.

We shook hands as if we were closing a business deal. "It's the best word in the English language," I said, using my professor voice.

Delia looked down. "Yeah," she said to herself. "I'm just sad about James. . . ."

All of a sudden I had an intense desire to get away from Delia and her whining about James. I wanted to go home, where I could think.

"Well, I guess we *both* lost the bet," I said, trying to bring our conversation to a close.

"You got that right." Delia's voice was a strange combination of sad and amused, but the expression on her face remained neutral.

To be honest, I didn't quite know what to make of the entire situation.

★　　★　　★

All the way home that night, I couldn't get Delia's plaintive wails about James out of my head. Understanding what she saw in that guy, aside from his male-model face, was beyond my comprehension.

But by the time I was undressed and lying in bed, one fact had become crystallized in my mind: I was distinctly irritated by Delia's eternal pining over James Suckface. Frankly, it was insulting.

Staring up at my ceiling, I thought of all the girls I'd kissed. All the worthwhile girls in school had gone out with me at one time or another, and Rebecca was the only one who'd made the move to end our relationship. But even with Rebecca, I knew that she'd broken up with me out of pride. She'd been hurt that I defended Delia, and she'd lashed out. Although I hadn't mentioned this to Delia, I was pretty sure that Rebecca would have taken me back if I'd asked. All week she'd been sending me smoldering looks across Mr. Maughn's homeroom.

But I didn't want to get back together with Rebecca, I reminded myself. I just wanted Delia to realize how many girls would have loved to have been in her shoes that night. And none of them would have burst into tears after I kissed them. Quite the opposite.

I sat up and punched my pillow. I needed to quit mooning around and take action. The very fact that I'd kissed Delia, and that I was now obsessing over her obsession with James, showed that I had too much time on my hands. As soon as I asked another girl out (with the clear understanding that I had no intention of falling in love), everything in my life would get back to normal.

In a flash, I remembered that Delia had suggested I ask Ellen for a date. Before that moment, I'd had less than no intention of asking out Ellen Frazier. But if Delia was so incredibly keen on the whole idea, then maybe I should. If nothing else, it would prove to her that while she was busy feeling miserable about that wimp she'd called a boyfriend, I was moving on with my life. And she certainly wouldn't have to worry about getting more kisses from me. I'd learned that lesson.

I closed my eyes, at last feeling that I could fall asleep. First thing in the morning, I would call Ellen Frazier. I would go out with Delia's friend and have a good time—even if it killed me.

Chapter Fifteen

Delia

I SPENT MOST of Saturday morning wandering aimlessly around the house. My parents had gone to a crafts show, and the house was deathly quiet. Later I was going to baby-sit Nina. But until then I had nothing to do. I realized that a teenager was in a pretty sad state when all she had to look forward to was an evening with a ten-year-old.

Around noon I sat down at my computer to work on a creative writing assignment. But my fingers just hovered over the keyboard. I had nothing to say. Thoughts about the night before swirled in my mind, but I couldn't make any sense of them. I felt as if I were suspended in space, waiting for something to happen—I just didn't know what that something was.

When the doorbell rang, I raced downstairs. At that point I would have been happy to sit down and chat with a door-to-door salesman. Anything to keep me occupied.

I immediately felt my mood brighten when I saw Ellen's car parked out front. I decided on the spot to tell her what had happened with Cain the night before.

"I've got some news that's going to blow you away," she said as soon as I opened the door.

"We're being invaded by aliens from outer space?" I responded, hanging up her navy blue pea coat.

"Aliens are nothing compared to what happened to me this morning," she said, her eyes bright.

We went into the kitchen, and I grabbed two diet colas from the refrigerator. "Don't keep me in suspense! Tell me everything."

She popped open her can of soda. "I was reading the paper this morning, just minding my own business. I mean, I was expecting nothing out of the day. Nothing."

"Get to the point already," I interrupted. "I can't wait."

"Cain called and asked me out—for tonight."

I coughed, choking on my soda. "You're kidding."

She shook her head. "Nope. We're going out to dinner."

"Wow." I felt as if I'd just been punched.

Ellen looked up at me, her eyes wide. "You don't care, do you? I mean, I figured you put in a good word for me and . . ."

I forced a smile onto my face. "I don't care. I'm just surprised he didn't mention it, that's all."

"You look sort of green," Ellen said, studying my face.

"Hey, I've always thought you two would make an awesome couple. I'm just so overcome with joy, I'm speechless."

Ellen grinned again. "Okay. I'll take your word for it. So, can I borrow something to wear?"

"We'll find exactly the right thing. When Cain sees you, Rebecca Foster will be just a dim memory."

Despite my words, I felt hollow. It was true that it had been my idea for Cain to ask Ellen out. But somehow I never thought he'd go through with it.

One thing was definite, though. I couldn't tell Ellen about kissing Cain. I could just imagine the two of them laughing about it over dinner. "Poor Delia," Cain would say. "She'll never get a boyfriend."

I shuddered. There was no way I could let either Cain or Ellen know that I was the least bit upset that they were going out.

"Let's go upstairs," I said, standing up. "We don't have a minute to waste."

"Thanks, Delia. I knew I could count on you for moral support." She gave me a quick hug, and when I looked at her face, I saw that she was beaming.

Once we were in my room, I started looking through my closet. I pulled out a green baby-doll dress and held it up to Ellen. "Try this on," I said.

"When you look at me, keep in mind that to-night I'll be wearing my Miracle Bra," Ellen said cheerfully. "Imagine an extra two inches up top."

I flopped on my bed and watched her undress.

"That bra is like your security blanket," I said.

She giggled. "How does this look?"

"Great." She'd put on the dress, which looked decidedly better on her than it did on me. "In fact, you can have it. The cut works much better on you."

Ellen turned around in front of the mirror. "Do you think Cain will like it, though?"

"Definitely."

Ellen went to my full-length mirror and studied her face. "I think I'm getting a zit on my chin."

"No, you're not," I said, willing myself to sound happy and encouraging.

Ellen sat down in my desk chair. "I'm sort of nervous," she confessed.

"Don't be. You're a million times cooler than anyone else Cain has ever dated."

Suddenly Ellen sat up straight. "Hey, you know Cain better than anyone else does. Do you have any tips about how I can get him to like me?"

I shut my eyes for a moment, thinking. How could I put everything I knew about Cain into a few meaningful phrases? In my mind I went over all the little details that I could tell her about my best friend. I took a deep breath, then opened my mouth.

"He hates pickles on his hamburger. Don't tell him you think you're fat. He doesn't care if you sing in the car—even if your voice sounds like a cow mooing. He likes impersonations. If you can't tell who he's trying to imitate, assume it's Elvis. When a little muscle next to his eye twitches, he's trying not to show you that he's angry. . . ."

Now that I'd started, I couldn't stop. I felt as if I'd opened the floodgates of a dam. Ellen was sitting in silence, watching me. She seemed to be listening, so I let myself continue.

"Green is his favorite color. He's a closet fan of disco music. At night he listens to talk radio. He hates girls who are superficial, although you'd never know that from looking at his *last* girlfriend. He'd rather die than work in a law office. He's funniest when—"

"Delia, are you all right?" Ellen asked suddenly. She was holding up her hand, signaling me to stop the torrent of words that was pouring forth.

I realized that I'd almost forgotten she was there. "What? Oh, sorry. I guess that was more information about Cain than you ever wanted to know."

Ellen was busily pushing back the cuticles of her fingernails. I saw her bite her lip, then she glanced up. "You're in love with Cain, aren't you?" She spoke quietly, but every word hammered in my brain.

"What?" I gasped. To have something to do, I grabbed a pillow and held it against my chest.

Ellen arched an eyebrow. "You heard me. I think you're in love with Cain Parson."

"That's the stupidest thing I ever heard," I said loudly, averting my gaze. "Don't be ridiculous."

"Delia, the way you're talking about him . . . it's like . . ."

"I am not in love with Cain. That's final." I knew my voice sounded strained, but I couldn't help it.

"If you're sure—"

"Sure I'm sure. Now take the dress and go get ready. I have somewhere to be."

Minutes later I closed the front door softly behind Ellen. I stood motionless in the hall, listening to the silence of the empty house. *I am not in love with Cain,* I told myself. As the words echoed in my mind I almost believed they were true.

Saturday night Nina was so hyper I practically had to drag her upstairs to go to bed. She'd been to Marcy Stein's boy-girl party the night before, and she seemed determined to give me each and every detail of the grand event.

"Then Peter Ross put an ice cube down my back," she said, reluctantly pulling on a flowered yellow nightgown.

"So what did you do?" I picked up her brush and motioned for her to sit on the edge of the bed.

"First I screamed. Then I got him back. Everybody was laughing so hard, I thought we were all going to pee in our pants." She giggled at the memory.

"Sit still," I said. "You've got a tangle." As I worked the brush through her long hair, I waited for her to continue.

"I haven't told you the best part," she said.

"There's more?" Despite my bad mood, I couldn't help smiling. Nina's enthusiasm for life tended to be infectious.

She nodded. "I'll only tell you if you promise not to tell my mom and dad," she said solemnly.

"Cross my heart."

She turned around to look at me, and I could see that she was bursting with her secret. "We played spin the bottle!"

"No!" I tried as hard as I could to sound scandalized. I was sure that Nina was hoping for a dramatic reaction.

"Yep! The boys were so gross, I thought I was going to barf."

"Who did you have to kiss?" I asked. I nudged her off the bed so I could pull back the covers.

"Peter Ross! Yuck." Nina scrunched up her face and stuck out her tongue.

I laughed. "I'm sure you'll live. You might even want to kiss him again someday."

She shook her head back and forth, making gagging sounds. "Not in a million years."

"If you say so," I said lightly, giving her a kiss good night. I reached over and switched off the lamp next to her bed.

As I started walking out of the room, Nina sat straight up in bed and turned the light back on. "Hey, Delia?"

"What?" I asked, putting my hands on my hips.

"Do you think I'll end up marrying Peter Ross? Since we kissed?"

"Yeah. And you'll live happily ever after." I turned the light back off, hoping she hadn't noticed the bitterness in my voice.

I left the room, sure that in about two minutes she'd fall sound asleep and dream all about "yucky" Peter Ross. I was glad I hadn't had the heart to tell her that after fifth grade, romance was all downhill. She'd find out soon enough.

Once I was downstairs, there wasn't much to keep me occupied. I finally grabbed a bag of pretzels and turned on MTV. As I bit ferociously into a pretzel I told myself that I hoped Cain and Ellen were having a good time. I really, really hoped they were having the ultimate time of their lives.

After an hour of music videos, I was bored, irritated, and overwhelmed with curiosity. I couldn't wait another second to find out how the date had gone. Checking my watch, I realized that Ellen must be home. How long could dinner take, anyway?

Ellen's phone rang three times before her mother answered. I knew Mrs. Frazier went to bed early, and her voice sounded groggy and slightly annoyed. If Ellen had been home, Mrs. Frazier wouldn't have bothered with the phone at all. Numbly I set the receiver back in its place.

Ellen wasn't home yet, which meant that she and Cain were still out together. The date had evidently been a success. Now there would be more dates. And more. Soon they'd be holding hands in public places. And I'd be a fifth wheel, alone and unwanted.

There was absolutely no way I could stand having Cain confide in me about how much he liked Ellen. Our friendship simply couldn't take that much pressure. But I wasn't about to stand in the way of his happiness—or Ellen's.

"I'll make a clean break," I said to the TV set. "It'll be the best solution for everybody."

Chapter Sixteen

Cain

"IS THAT DELIA'S dress?" I asked Ellen suddenly. She looked down, smiling. "Yeah. She gave it to me."

"Why?" I knew I wasn't being very polite, but I couldn't imagine why Delia would give away her green dress. It was one of my favorites—and I couldn't help noticing that the dress looked a lot better on Deels.

"I guess she was sick of wearing it," Ellen said, shrugging.

"She just frustrates me so much," I said, as if Ellen weren't there.

We were sitting at a table in Anthony's Pasta House, and my head felt as if it were about to explode. I'd made it all the way through appetizers and entrees without uttering Delia's name, making a huge effort to be attentive and see Ellen as someone

I could date. But by the time the waiter brought our coffee, I knew a romance with Ellen was a lost cause. In my eyes, she was Delia's friend. I thought she was a great person, but whenever I looked at her, I saw Delia. Now I was letting myself talk about what had been on my mind all day—Delia Byrne.

"I assume we're talking about Delia now?" she asked, arching an eyebrow.

"Yeah."

"I think you frustrate her, too," Ellen said, her voice serious. She took a sip of coffee, waiting for me to say something.

"I just love her so much." I poured more cream into my cup and stirred absently.

"She loves you, too," Ellen said, sighing.

"Really?"

"Yes, really." Ellen paused. "And to think I actually thought I'd been asked out on a date tonight. Looks like what you really needed was a therapist." Shaking her head, she laughed to herself.

All of a sudden I realized what a jerk I was. "Ellen, I'm sorry. I didn't mean to go on and on about Delia. Let's talk about something else. Like, ah, where do you want to go to college?"

She laughed again softly. "Cain, don't even try to pretend that you're interested in where I want to go to college. To be honest, you're not that good an actor."

"I'm that transparent?" I asked, chagrined.

"From the second you picked me up, your mind has been a thousand miles away." She leaned back in her chair, folding and unfolding a paper napkin.

"I thought if we went on a date, I'd forget how . . ." I wasn't sure what I was trying to say.

"You'd forget that you're in love with Delia?" Ellen asked wryly.

"No!" I protested quickly. "I mean, I just broke up with Rebecca and everything—"

"Spare me," Ellen interrupted. "You and Delia are in love, and everyone else at Jefferson High has known it for years. If you would just face up to reality and let yourselves be together, the rest of us could go on with our lives."

My heart was beating furiously, and I could barely catch my breath. "Do you really think Delia's in love with me?"

She set down her coffee cup with a bang. "Cain, I *know* she is. You should have seen her today. She was pretending she didn't care that you'd asked me out. But I could see actual *tears* glistening in her eyes."

"Are you telling me the truth?" My mouth felt dry, and I reached for my glass of ice water.

Ellen rubbed her temples. "Think about it, Cain. You know I've had a really stupid crush on you for, like, the last two years. Now I'm finally on what at least *started* as a date with you. Do you really and truly believe I would spend tonight saying I thought you and Delia were meant to be together if I wasn't being one hundred percent honest?" She finished her speech and signaled to the waiter for our check.

"I get your point," I said, almost to myself.

"Good. Now let's get out of here. I'm sure you

want to go home and think about Delia."

"Ellen, please promise me you won't tell Delia one word of what I've said tonight." I held my breath, praying she'd agree to keep her mouth shut.

"I promise," she said.

I let out my breath in a relieved sigh. "How can I thank you for being so cool?" I asked. "The sky's the limit."

She gestured toward the bill on the table. "Tell you what. I'll let you pay for my dinner."

"Done," I said. Of course, I would have paid for her dinner anyway.

"And could you do me one more favor?" she asked, putting on her coat.

"Anything."

"Never, *ever* ask me out on another date." She grinned, and I saw her eyes sparkle with laughter.

I took her hand in mine and gave her a kiss on the forehead. "You know, Ellen Frazier, you're all right."

I was whistling as we left the restaurant. In fact, I sang all the way home.

The second I walked into my house, I bounded up the stairs to my room. In my head I was already dialing Delia's phone number. We had a lot to talk about.

But when I sat down on my bed, the phone perched next to me, I felt suddenly deflated. Talking to Ellen, everything had seemed so simple. Now that I was alone, my feelings were much more complicated. Delia and I had been best friends for three years. Our relationship was set up a certain way, and I'd never given serious thought to changing the dynamic.

I put the phone back on my nightstand and walked over to the big bulletin board on my wall. The whole board was covered with pictures from my first three years of high school. Almost half of the photographs featured Delia. A big one in the center caught my eye.

My mom had taken the picture during the spring of our freshman year. Delia and I had been working, along with a bunch of other people, at a car wash. I thought back, remembering that we'd been trying to raise money for a local children's hospital. At about three o'clock in the afternoon, business had slowed down. We were all exhausted, and everyone had gotten a little cranky.

Suddenly I'd grabbed a hose and sprayed Delia. She'd responded by dumping a bucket of soapy water on my head. After that, everyone had gotten involved. For the next few minutes water and soap flew everywhere, and we were all laughing hysterically.

When I'd finally put the hose down, I saw that my mom had brought our old station wagon to be washed. She had a camera in her hand, and she was standing several yards away—out of firing range. Just the moment before, Delia had come over and given me a high five. I still remembered the way our hands had slipped off each other because they were covered in soap. My mom had caught the moment on film.

Even standing alone in my room, the image made me laugh out loud. Laughing and slapping me on the hand, Delia was the epitome of herself. It was as though her whole essence leaped straight out of the picture and tugged at my heart.

My gaze moved to the other photographs on the bulletin board. Some of them were of Andrew and me, playing basketball or doing other guy things. But my favorites were all of Delia and me—with my grandmother, on horseback, building a snowman.

What if I told Delia my real feelings, and she didn't feel the same way? I'd be humiliated, not to mention minus one best friend. Our easy banter and shared confidences would be gone forever.

Or what if Delia and I did start dating, and the relationship ended up like the others? There was no guarantee that our love would last. She could meet someone she liked better, or decide that I was a terrible kisser, or realize that my jokes weren't funny after all. My heart would break, and I'd lose everything that mattered most to me in the world.

Sighing heavily, I lay down on my bed. The silent phone seemed to mock me, and I felt like throwing it against the wall. Instead I picked up the receiver and dialed the first six digits of the Byrnes' phone number.

But just as I was about to press the last number, I stopped. For several numb minutes I sat motionless, staring at the Michael Jordan poster on my wall. I couldn't do it, I realized. I couldn't risk my friendship. The stakes were just too high.

Without bothering to undress, I switched off the light and sank into bed. "Delia will never know how I feel," I vowed to myself. "Never."

Chapter Seventeen

Delia

I WOKE UP Sunday morning with a splitting headache. Downstairs I could hear cheerful voices as my parents argued over whether or not to get a new water heater. I groaned and shoved my face into my pillow as the last twenty-four torturous hours came rushing back to me. Ellen and Cain. Cain and Ellen. Delia and nobody. It must have been around five-thirty in the morning (yes, I had lain awake most of the night, staring at the cracks on my ceiling) that I'd realized exactly why I felt so horrible. Now I said the words out loud for the first time, just to see if they were still true.

"I'm in love with Cain," I whispered. "And he's not in love with me." Saying that was even harder than thinking it. I brushed a few tears off my face. It wasn't even ten o'clock yet and I was crying. Wow, what a great life, I thought sarcastically. I rolled over in bed, forcing myself to repeat the truth over and over again.

When I couldn't stand my own thoughts any longer, I dragged myself out of bed. It was still early, but there was no point in putting off the inevitable. I had to break all of my ties with Cain, and I had to do it that day.

I put on my oldest pair of jeans and dug out a faded Jefferson High sweatshirt. For good measure, I stuck a baseball cap on my head and slid my feet into a pair of beat-up moccasins. As I struggled to get all of my hair into a scrunchie, I decided that I'd have my hair shorn, even if Cain didn't insist on it when I lost the bet. Why bother with my appearance? From then on, I was going to be hanging out with my parents every weekend anyway.

From the hall closet I retrieved a sagging cardboard box, which I set in the middle of my unmade bed. Slowly I made my way around my room, running my hands over different mementos of my high-school years. Most of them reminded me of Cain in one way or another, and I felt fresh tears roll down my cheeks. I had to get rid of everything. Even the smallest souvenir that reminded me of our friendship would be torture to have around.

I carefully placed the teddy bear Cain had won for me at a carnival our sophomore year into the box. I'd named the bear Chuckles, because Cain always made me laugh. The stuffed animal was followed by a pair of dangly silver earrings—Cain's present to me on my sixteenth birthday.

I went to the wall by my desk and took down the framed photograph of Cain and me at a car wash. As I studied our smiling, soap-covered faces one more time, my heart constricted painfully. After dropping the picture into the box, I rummaged through my dresser drawers. I'd accumulated about a million of Cain's T-shirts over the last three years, and I'd never bothered to return them. "He'll be psyched to get these back," I whispered, holding a black concert T-shirt up to my face.

After what seemed like just a few minutes, the box was full. I glanced around my room, which now looked bare and impersonal. Most of my life had been placed into a cardboard box. There was nothing left.

I picked up the box and slouched toward the door of my room. "So long, Chuckles," I said. "It's been nice knowing you."

Mrs. Parson didn't try to stop me when I pushed past her and headed for the stairs. I was on a mission, and no one was going to stand in my way. The stairs seemed to go on forever, and the heavy weight of the box made my arm and back muscles ache.

At the door of Cain's room, I dropped the box. The thump echoed through the house, announcing my presence. Then I knocked loudly on Cain's door, not caring that his parents had probably decided I was a lunatic.

"What?" Cain yelled from inside. His voice was so familiar, so *him,* that I almost backed down and made a go of reconciling my mixed-up emotions.

But I shook my head firmly, remembering that I'd warned myself against this very temptation. I'd known that confronting Cain would be hard, but there was no other option.

"It's me," I called sharply, willing my voice not to crack. I opened the door and shoved the box into his room with my foot. Then I walked inside, crossing my arms in front of me.

"What's up?" Cain asked, looking both sleepy and bewildered. His hair was rumpled and his blankets were twisted around his torso. Even in that state, Cain was gorgeous. He could have been the poster boy for a mattress ad campaign.

"I brought all of your stuff," I said flatly. I had no idea how to begin explaining that we couldn't be friends anymore. "I, uh, realized that I had a lot of your T-shirts."

He glanced at the digital clock next to his bed. "You felt compelled to bring me my *T-shirts* at ten o'clock on a Sunday morning?"

"I had to," I said, as if I'd just explained everything. "I'm sure you're tired after your big date with Ellen, so I'll let you get back to sleep." I turned on my heel, ready to flee.

"Wait!" Cain said, wide awake now. "Will you please tell me *what's* going on? You're not making any sense."

I studied the floor, desperately trying to think of what I should say. There seemed to be some holes in my plan to make a clean break from Cain. "We can't be friends anymore," I said finally.

Once the words were out, I couldn't stop the tears that poured from my eyes. Cain was frowning, and he looked so lovable and trusting that I wanted nothing more than to throw myself in his arms and beg him to fall in love with me. But then my gaze rested on his lips, and I imagined him kissing Ellen. They'd probably spent all of dessert making out in the restaurant. The image sent a stabbing pain through my heart.

"Why not?" Cain asked, his voice high and shaky.

"Things between us just aren't the same," I said between sobs. "I don't know how else to explain it."

He was silent, staring at me with his mouth hanging open. I wished the floor would open and swallow me up, but nothing happened—not even a quick bolt of lightning.

"You and Ellen will make a great couple," I said. "I wish you both all the happiness in the world."

"Ellen and I? We're not—"

"Don't say another word!" I shouted. "I don't want to hear about it."

"But Delia, this is insane. Worse than insane!" He'd gotten out of bed and was walking toward me.

"I'm sorry, Cain. I've failed as a friend, and I know it. But please, don't say anything. Just leave me alone—forever."

I backed out of the room and slammed the door behind me. I stumbled down the stairs, tears and heartache blurring my vision.

At the bottom of the stairs I turned toward the front door, ignoring a very alarmed-looking Mrs. Parson. I heard Cain shouting my name, but I blocked out the sound of his voice.

Once outside, I raced toward my mother's brown Toyota, which I'd parked in the driveway. Backing out, I saw Cain standing at the front door. He was waving his arms and jumping up and down. Bravely, I looked away.

I sped down the quiet street, leaving my heart behind.

Despite the freezing-cold day, I rolled down my car window and let the air wash over me. I felt as if I were suffocating, and the feel of the wind was a welcome relief. I was driving aimlessly, praying that as the miles between Cain and me grew, I would feel like a human being again.

Briefly I turned on the car radio. The low, melodious tones of the deejay filled the car, and I sank back in my seat, grateful to hear another voice. With any luck, I could push the sound of Cain calling to me out of my mind.

"And this golden oldie, 'Let's Fall in Love,' goes out to Rachel from Andrew. He says he had a great time last night, and he's glad he finally got up the nerve to ask you to be his girl," the deejay said.

I switched off the radio, laughing bitterly. The irony was overpowering, and I had to pull the Toyota into a parking lot and collect myself. What were the chances that I would turn on the radio and hear a dedication from Andrew Rice to Rachel Hall? It seemed that everyone at Jefferson High was finally getting lucky in love. Everyone but me.

I rested my head on the steering wheel, taking deep, gasping breaths. I would never go to my senior prom. I would never have a date to the all-night graduation party. Ellen and I wouldn't double to the Winter Ball. Cain and I wouldn't exchange Christmas presents or go sledding. From then on, I would walk through the halls of Jefferson High, a mere ghost of my former self.

I started fantasizing about taking the high-school equivalency exam and leaving Jefferson early. I would move to another town, get a job, and start a whole new life. I pictured myself living in New York, dancing in some terrible off-Broadway musical. Then I envisioned a new life out in the Midwest. I could move to Nebraska and become a farmhand. Or I could drive to California and become a hippie. Maybe I could even assume a new identity—I'd call myself Rainbow or Moonbeam.

Finally I sat up and brushed the tears from my eyes. For the time being, I was plain old Delia Byrne. And I was miserable. My parents weren't going to let me move out of state or do any of that. They were going to force me to suffer through my pitiful existence, enduring one lonely day after another.

I turned on the ignition and pulled out of the parking lot. After driving for I didn't know how long, I found myself in front of the Tivoli Theater. The Tivoli was an old movie house that showed classics on Saturdays and Sundays. When I saw that *Casablanca* was starting at one o'clock, I parked my mom's car in the deserted lot.

Casablanca was the movie Cain and I had watched over the phone together last September. Back then, our feelings for each other had been pure and uncomplicated. If only I could have turned back the clock, undoing all of the time that had passed since that innocent night.

When I bought the ticket, the woman in the ticket booth looked at me strangely. "The show doesn't start for another forty-five minutes," she said. "You might want to come back later."

I shook my head, realizing I had nowhere else to go. An empty movie theater was as good a place as any to be alone.

"I'll wait," I answered, knowing there were tears in my voice.

"Okay, hon," she answered kindly. "Go on in."

Without any people, the theater felt eerie and surreal. But I sat down anyway. Worn out, I closed my eyes, blocking out the sight of the rows and rows of empty seats. Whether I had to wait forty-five minutes or a lifetime was inconsequential. Life had lost its meaning.

Chapter Eighteen

Cain

I STOOD IN the doorway until Delia's car had disappeared around the corner. My mom was standing behind me, looking even more shocked than I felt.

"What was that about?" she asked.

"It's a long story," I said, sighing.

Without another word, I climbed the stairs to my room and put the cardboard box Delia had brought onto my bed. With a sinking heart, I began examining the box's contents, item by item. When I found Chuckles at the bottom, I held him to my chest and burrowed beneath the covers.

I didn't know what had come over Delia. Was it possible that Ellen had told her what I'd said the night before? I shook my head. I'd believed Ellen when she said she would keep the secret.

I went over everything that had happened since Labor Day. Although we'd been fighting more than

174

usual (a lot more), I'd never thought Delia would want to quit being my best friend. To me, the idea of us not being friends was as foreign as the idea of not breathing. We were meant to be together, and now she was tearing us apart. Why?

With all my heart, I wanted to believe she was jealous of Ellen. But it had been Delia's idea that I ask her friend out in the first place. She'd wanted me to get over Rebecca and move on with my life. And it had been Delia who was pining over James, acting as if her whole world had come to an end when he went back to Tanya. Plus, when I'd kissed her on Friday, she'd been the one to pull away. As I remembered her sobbing over James, I felt sick to my stomach.

Throughout the morning, I picked up the various objects that Delia had dropped off. Every time I looked down at the stuffed bear's fuzzy brown face, a fresh wave of pain washed over me. Delia had begged me to leave her alone, and there was nothing I could do about it.

Finally I got angry. Who did Delia think she was? Since when did she make all the decisions in our friendship? I picked up the phone. I was going to force her to talk to me, even if I had to go to her house and barricade myself in her room.

I hung up when her answering machine picked up. Somehow the idea of leaving a desperate message—with her possibly in the room listening to it—was too much to bear. I couldn't force Delia to talk to me. She'd just get mad and say I was being a bully. All I could do was . . . exactly nothing.

I was startled when the phone rang. But I grabbed the receiver on the first ring, hoping against hope that Delia had come to her senses.

"Yo, Parson," I heard Andrew say brightly.

"Hey, Andrew." My heart had already sunk to my feet, and I was rapidly trying to think up an excuse to get off the phone as quickly as possible.

"I finally took the plunge, man." He sounded positively ecstatic. "I did it."

"What do you mean?" I asked, massaging my aching neck with one hand.

"*Rachel*. Last night I took Rachel on a date. It was incredible. I just woke up in the morning and said to myself, 'Rice, today you're going to be a man and call the girl who's got you acting like a crazy person.' So I called her, she said yes, and the rest is romantic history."

"I take it you two had a good time," I said, trying to keep the cynicism out of my voice.

"Dude, it was like we were made for each other. And you know what the best part is?" he asked.

"What?" I squeezed Chuckles as hard as I could, willing myself to be happy for Andrew and Rachel.

"She told me that she's been in love with me this entire semester. Is that great, or what?"

"It's awesome," I said.

I couldn't believe that Andrew Rice, of all people, was in love. He'd always been the guy to scoff at me and my notion of searching for Ms. Right. Now he was babbling like an idiot, sounding happier than I'd ever heard him.

"Do you want to know what I did this morning?"

"Do tell."

Andrew didn't seem to notice that I wasn't enjoying our conversation as much as he was. "I called up one of the radio stations and got the deejay to do a dedication. Then I called Rachel and told her to turn on the radio. We both stayed on the phone, not even talking, just waiting for my song to come on." Andrew sighed contentedly.

"Sounds like you've fallen pretty hard," I commented, unsure of how to tell him that listening to him talk about declarations of love was like having a knife twisted in my heart.

"I even asked her to the Winter Ball," Andrew continued. "Hey, maybe we can double with you and whoever."

"Somehow I don't think I'll be going."

"Cain, of course you're going. If nothing else, you and Delia can go together. You're both single—and most people think you guys are going out, anyway."

I heard myself laugh maniacally. Talking to Andrew for one more second might drive me to jump out the window. "Listen, man, my mom's calling me. But I'm really psyched for you and Rachel. Keep up the good work."

I hung up the phone before he could say anything else. I was only seventeen, and my life had come to nothing but pain and loneliness. Lying there, I wasn't sure how much more I could take.

★　　　★　　　★

177

I had no idea how much time had passed when my mother stuck her head in my door. It could have been seconds, hours, or days.

"Dad and I are going to an auction," she said. "Want to come with us?"

I shoved Chuckles under my blanket and shook my head. "I think I'll just hang out here for a while."

My mother smiled her most maternal smile, making me feel like I was about five years old. "Okay, sweetie. But don't stay in bed all day. It's not healthy." She shut the door behind her, and I pulled Chuckles out from his hiding place.

When I heard the garage door open, I rolled out of bed. In the bathroom I made a vague attempt to brush my teeth and wash my face. But even the thought of brushing my hair seemed like too much of an effort.

Still feeling as if I were moving in a vacuum, I went down to the kitchen and poured myself a cup of black coffee. Then I leafed indifferently through the paper, hoping to get my mind off Delia.

I read through the sports section, but as soon as I'd finished looking at the scores, I realized that I couldn't remember who'd won the football game. I also realized that I really didn't care.

I turned to the art section. Maybe a movie would offer some escape from my grim reality. My gaze fell on a huge ad for *Casablanca*. The film was playing at the Tivoli, and the first showing started at one o'clock. My thoughts flashed back to the last time I'd seen that film. Delia had already been in bed when I'd called her, but she'd gotten up and watched the whole film.

178

I glanced at the clock. The movie started in fifteen minutes. I raced to the front door, put on my jacket, and grabbed my keys. Then I automatically went to the phone to call Delia and see if she wanted to go with me.

The second my hand touched the receiver, I jerked it back. For a brief moment I'd forgotten that the whole point of going to see a movie was to keep myself from thinking about what had happened that morning. I walked slowly away from the phone, feeling nauseated. According to Delia, I could never call her again. I'd have to get used to going to old movies alone. None of my other friends understood the appeal of a classic black-and-white film.

Driving to the theater, I realized that watching Humphrey Bogart and Ingrid Bergman was not going to take my mind off Delia. If anything, I'd cry when the movie got to the part where Sam played "As Time Goes By" for Ilsa.

I bought a ticket anyway. Nothing was going to keep me from thinking about Delia, so I figured I might as well be depressed in the haven of a dark theater.

"Are you meeting someone here?" the lady at the booth asked me as she gave me my change.

"Nope. Far from it," I answered.

She shrugged. "There must be something in the air today," she said, almost to herself.

"There must be," I agreed, not knowing what she was talking about but not caring, either.

Since I was already late, I went to the concession stand for popcorn. I hadn't eaten a thing all day, and my stomach was rumbling. I wasn't sure I could manage a whole tub of movie-theater popcorn, but I asked for extra butter, just in case.

Inside, the small theater was only about half full. Humphrey Bogart was on the screen, and there was music playing in the background. At that moment I could really relate to Bogart, who was playing Rick. The character had lost his one true love, and now he was forced to live out a meaningless existence. He was always cool and untouchable, because nothing mattered to him. I decided I was going to be like that from now on—a detached macho man who glided through life unfettered by emotions or desires.

Lost in the tragedy of my thoughts, I waited for my eyes to adjust to the dim lighting. Then I moved slowly forward, looking for the least densely populated area of seats. I wanted to be as alone as possible during my mental breakdown.

When I got a third of the way down the aisle, my heart started pumping in my chest. The back of a familiar dark head was just a few rows in front of me. Almost dropping my popcorn, I stopped in my tracks.

With one hand, I rubbed first one eye, then the other. I was sure that I was hallucinating. What were the chances that Delia was sitting right before my very eyes—almost as if she knew I'd come and find her?

I closed my eyes for a moment, and when I opened them, she was still there. As I started walking again I couldn't suppress the feeling that, unlike Rick's, my romance was about to have a very happy ending.

Chapter Nineteen

Delia

INGRID BERGMAN HADN'T even appeared onscreen yet, and I was already swallowing back the tears. Usually my eyes stayed dry at least until Rick found Sam playing "As Time Goes By" on the piano for Ilsa. Thinking about her strength, I became determined not to act like an idiot. Ilsa never would have cried her way through an entire movie—she hadn't even cried her way through an entire war.

I patted my eyes with my sweatshirt, sitting up straighter in my seat. Unbidden, my thoughts turned to Cain. But instead of focusing on the way our friendship had ended, I thought about all the great times we'd had together.

A montage of Cain and me together flitted through my mind, and I smiled. First there was the memory of the two of us tipping a canoe at Gambler's Pond. Then I remembered when he'd shown up at my door dressed as the Easter Bunny. And I laughed out loud at the memory of Cain somersaulting down a mountain on a school ski trip. He'd stood up after his tumble and bowed deeply to a bunch of surprised skiers.

And then there was the image of us kissing. I could almost feel his warm lips on mine, his fingers running through my hair. And when we'd danced at homecoming, I'd felt as if we were in our own private world. His arms had held me close, and for long minutes I'd forgotten that I was supposed to be in love with James.

What a joke, I thought. I'd never been in love with James. I wasn't sure I'd even been in *like* with James. I'd mistaken the desire for a boyfriend with true love. Now the idea that I'd shed a tear over him and Tanya seemed laughable.

I was so lost in memories of Cain that I didn't even notice someone coming up beside me. No one else was sitting in my row, but suddenly I felt a person take the seat next to mine. Out of nowhere, the hairs on the back of my neck stood up, and it seemed that a jolt of electricity was coursing through my whole body. Even before I turned my head, I knew the person beside me was Cain.

"Did somebody order popcorn?" he whispered in my ear.

I stared at him dumbly, my head spinning. It was almost as if I'd conjured him up by thinking about him with such intense concentration. Now he was less than inches away, and even in the darkness of the theater, I could read the warmth in his eyes. I took in his uncombed hair, the shadow of his beard. Looking down, I noticed that he was wearing mismatched sneakers on his feet. *He looks even worse than I do,* I thought, my pulse racing.

I couldn't speak, but I reached into his tub of popcorn and took a big handful. Then I turned back to the screen, afraid that I was going to burst into tears. I didn't know what I was feeling, but I was glad that Cain was close. With him there, the pain of losing our friendship was dulled. For the next hour and a half, at least, we would be together.

For what seemed like forever, we were both rigid in our seats, not daring to look at each other. Days and nights passed in *Casablanca,* but for me the film went by in a haze. Cain's nearness was occupying every part of my mind.

We weren't touching, but the heat emanating from his body seemed to reach out and envelop me. At one point we both put our hands in the popcorn. When our skin made contact we sprang apart, each edging as far as we could to the side.

But during the last scene of the movie, our shoulders and arms were pressed together, and I almost couldn't breathe. I'd never been so acutely aware of another human being. But he wasn't just another human being. He was Cain—my best friend and my one true love.

As I listened to Humphrey Bogart say, "We'll always have Paris," tears glistened in my eyes for the first time since Cain had sat down beside me.

Suddenly I felt his breath on my cheek, and I tilted my head toward him. Every nerve ending of my body quivered, waiting for something to happen.

"We'll always have . . . ," Cain whispered in my ear. I thought he was going to finish the sentence with "Paris," but he didn't. "Forever," he finished.

I reached out and took his hand, clasping his fingers as tightly as I could. When I turned my face toward his, he used his other hand to gently trace the line of my lips. I was sure that everyone in the theater could hear the beating of my heart, but I didn't care.

"I love you," I whispered.

"I love you," he whispered back.

Our lips met as the credits rolled. I kissed him with all of the pent-up longing of the last few weeks, months, years. Cain's kisses were equally passionate, and I felt that for the first time ever, we truly understood each other.

As we remained locked together, our kiss ever deepening, I completely forgot where we were. Nothing and no one else mattered. The world consisted of Cain and me, me and Cain. Everything else was just a mirage, evaporating quickly into thin air.

Without warning, the lights came on. Still we kissed. Not until everyone in the theater broke into spontaneous applause and cheering did we break apart. We looked at each other guiltily, then burst out laughing. A loud whistle from someone walking up the aisle made us laugh even harder. But we didn't stop looking at each other. We were lost in the absolute perfectness of the moment.

After everyone else had filed out of the theater, Cain took my hand and pulled me from my seat. We walked up the narrow aisle with our arms wrapped around each other, not caring that we couldn't take a step without bumping into each other.

In the bright lobby, the woman from the ticket booth stood with her hands on her hips. "I had a feeling!" she exclaimed, seeing us emerge. "Like I said, there's something in the air."

We walked out into the street, smiling and giggling like fools. *Fools in love*, I thought blissfully.

Suddenly Cain stopped and threw his arms around me. I hugged him back, squeezing him as tightly as I could.

"Hey, Deels?" he said.

"What?" I brushed his hair away from his face, loving its silky feel against my fingertips.

"Do you have a date for the Winter Ball?" he asked. "There's a certain bet I need to win."

I pulled him even closer, lightly kissing every part of his face that I could reach. Then I laughed and gave him a gentle punch in the arm. "I think you mean there's a certain bet *I* need to win," I said, looking into his eyes.

Cain's eyes grew serious, and he placed his hands on either side of my head. "I think we've *both* won," he murmured softly.

Then he kissed me, and I'm not clear on what happened next. All I remember is that the night ended with hot chocolate and a fireplace. You can probably guess the rest. . . .

Do you ever wonder about falling in love? About members of the opposite sex? Do you need a little friendly advice but have no one to turn to? Well, that's where we come in . . . Jenny and Jake. Send us those questions you're dying to ask, and we'll give you the straight scoop on life and love.

DEAR JAKE

Q: *I've got a huge problem. I think my boyfriend Scott isn't into me anymore. Most of the time when we're together, Scott and I have a great time. But every so often he tells me that he thinks his friend, Michael, would be a much better boyfriend for me. Of course I'd rather date Scott than Michael—that's why Scott's my boyfriend and not anyone else. But even though we go out together all the time, I still feel as if Scott's trying to get rid of me, and it really hurts. Why does Scott keep doing this?*

VS, Mason, TN

A: First things first, I don't think Scott would keep asking you out if he didn't like you. Next, you should ask yourself the following questions . . . Do you spend a lot of time with Michael? Is Michael really cute? Popular? Smart? Flirtatious? If so, could Scott just be insecure? Jealous of his friend? Do you give Scott any reason to think you like Michael better than you like him? If you answered yes to any of these questions, you need to sit Scott down, once and for all, and tell him that you're totally into him. That you are *not* interested in Michael—or anyone else for that matter. Have a real heart to heart with your one and only—and tell him how strong your love is. This lack of communication can potentially destroy a great romance.

DEAR JENNY

Q: *Ever since I began dating Frank, my best friend Erin has become a different person. She's always in a bad mood and lately she's been totally ignoring me. It's obvious that she isn't happy for me, and that really hurts. I want to continue my friendship with Erin. Is there any way to stay friends without getting rid of my boyfriend?*

RM, Atlanta, GA

A: Before you put all the blame on Erin, you should think about the way you've been acting toward her. Does Erin have a boyfriend? If not, do you talk about anything but how happy you are with Frank? Have you stopped going to her house after school? Maybe she's jealous of the time you're now spending with Frank. Or maybe she's just jealous of the fact that you have a boyfriend and she doesn't. Irregardless, you could make an extra effort to spend time with Erin—special time without Frank hanging along. Go to the movies together, grab a pizza, anything. Just let her know she's still your friend and you miss her. Apologize for neglecting her and work together to get around the boyfriend problem. She'll appreciate your efforts, and the two of you should be back on the road to friendship in no time.

Do you have questions about love? Write to:

Jenny Burgess or Jake Korman
c/o Daniel Weiss Associates
33 West 17th Street
New York, NY 10011